A Different Drummer

A Different Drummer

Edna M. Wilkinson

Copyright © 2006 by Edna M. Wilkinson.

ISBN 10:   Softcover   1-4257-2680-1

ISBN 13:   Softcover   978-1-4257-2680-5

All rights reserved. No part of this book may be reproduced or transmitted in any form or by any means, electronic or mechanical, including photocopying, recording, or by any information storage and retrieval system, without permission in writing from the copyright owner.

This book was printed in the United States of America.

To order additional copies of this book, contact:
Xlibris Corporation
1-888-795-4274
www.Xlibris.com
Orders@Xlibris.com

Contents

Foreword 9
Chapter 1   The Pregnancy 12
Chapter 2   In The Beginning 17
Chapter 3   The Early Years 20
Chapter 4   Life In The Country 22
Chapter 5   School Begins 29
Chapter 6   More Steps Up The Mountain 34
Chapter 7   A Crisis Of A Different Kind 40
Chapter 8   A Special Friendship 49
Chapter 9   Everything Happens For A Reason 53
Chapter 10 A Young Man Blossoms 57
Chapter 11 A Troubled Teen 63
Chapter 12 Considering Options 69
Chapter 13 A Time To Be Merry 72
Chapter 14 Time Flies 75

For Todd, without whom this story would never have been written.

"How do I love thee? Let me count the ways..."
Elizabeth Barrett Browning

Bluebirds and Rainbows

You see, there's this big rocky mountain
That life tells me I'll have to climb;
And I don't know if I'll ever make it,
If I do, it will take a long time.
But I'll just keep on climbing and climbing
'Till I stand in the warm golden sun,
And the whole world will be mine forever
When the top of the mountain I've won.

If I can climb to the top of this mountain,
I can wipe all the clouds from my sky;
I can sit on the edge of a rainbow
And watch all the bluebirds fly by.
I believe there's a bright new tomorrow
That's coming for people like me;
If I can climb to the top of this mountain,
There'll be bluebirds and rainbows to see.

Edna M. Wilkinson

Foreword

As a stay-at-home mother with ten children, I was rarely afforded the time to sit down and enjoy daytime television thirty years ago. But when a daughter-in-law called one morning in 1975 to inform me that a well-known talk show was featuring guests with Down's Syndrome, I rushed to turn on our black and white t.v.

As the minutes passed, I became increasingly disappointed, for what I was watching was in distinct contrast to my own experience with my Down's son.

I saw a twenty-one year-old youth who had progressed through the school system and now attended college. His father was at his side, and answered most of the questions asked by the interviewer. The youth was well-dressed and had excellent manners. When asked what his future plans were he replied, "Not sure."

I watched and listened to a four year-old Down's girl who read aloud from a story book. Also present were a sixteen year-old girl and a one year-old baby. The sixteen year-old had been through surgery to alter facial features and reduce the size of her tongue.

I listened to proud parents describing the many accomplishments of their Down's children, and was amazed. I was aware of borderline cases where some Down's Syndrome people progressed much further than others, however their numbers seemed relatively few in comparison to the majority of people with Down's. It occurred to me that if I had viewed that program with no prior knowledge of the condition, I would have been left with a very unrealistic impression.

I was hoping the program would offer something helpful, new information perhaps, and new methods of coping. At that time there was little in way of support groups for parents of children with Down's Syndrome.

A week after viewing the aforementioned talk show, I watched a television movie that focused on a Down's boy who excelled in reading and mathematics in his special education class.

Both of these programs filled me with self-doubt. Had I been doing something wrong? Though I am happy for those parents who see their Down's child progress at an almost "normal" pace, it hasn't been my experience with my son.

When I began writing this book, Todd was nineteen years old, and attended a special school for the mentally handicapped. He was unable to tie his shoes, and will probably never be able to tie them, so he's always worn footwear with Velcro fasteners.

He doesn't manage buttons well, so his shirts are mostly the pull-on type. His communication skills are minimal, although the immediate family understands him most of the time.

He knows a few words by sight, and is able to count to ten or twelve. Money means nothing to him, except for the fact that he knows he must have some if he wants to buy something at the store. That "something" usually turns out to be potato chips and a soda pop. After making a purchase, he refuses to leave until the cashier puts his merchandise in a bag.

His greatest passion is music, and he listens to it for hours at a time. In his younger days he would disappear into his room after school, close the door against any and all intruders, and then turn the volume on the radio as high as it would go. When his younger nieces and nephews would come to visit, he didn't often allow them into his sanctuary.

He has several favourite television programs. They include "The Waltons", "The Brady Bunch", "Good Times", "Happy Days", and "Star Trek".

At the special needs school he attended, the accent was mainly on life skills and personal hygiene. Though he must always be supervised, he is good at washing and drying dishes, setting and clearing the table after a meal, and preparing a simple snack.

Particularly in his younger days, Todd was known to be affectionate and loving. As a matter of fact, it took a long time to teach him that it wasn't proper to kiss every female he saw! Normal male instinct, perhaps, but it could be embarrassing while shopping. He'd point to the cashier saying, "Her cute"! Thank goodness that phase seems to be over.

So we take each day as it comes, and I'm never quite sure what will happen next. Perhaps it's just as well we aren't allowed to glimpse the future. If we were, we might turn tail and run. I'm sort of tagging along behind him, trying to keep up, never quite sure if I'm doing the right thing.

Perhaps I should start at the beginning of our story to give you a true picture of our life together.

Chapter 1

The Pregnancy

I became pregnant for the tenth time at the age of forty-one. Perhaps because bearing a child was not a new experience for me, having already given birth to five daughters and four sons, I was expecting another normal pregnancy culminating in the birth of a healthy baby. There was certainly no warning throughout those nine months to alter my expectations, and my gynecologist assured me that everything was proceeding smoothly.

Labour began on the evening of our twenty-fifth wedding anniversary, and my husband drove me the six miles to the hospital. I remember saying to Frank, "What a way to celebrate!"

These hasty nighttime trips were a familiar occurrence for us, a normal part of life. And as had been the case with most of my previous deliveries, my husband left for home the minute I was safely in the nurse's care. After all, there were nine other children waiting to be attended to!

Frank usually received word of the arrival of a new addition to the family by telephone after the delivery. This was one father who never paced the floor of the waiting room, biting his nails and consuming endless cups of black coffee. I liked it that way, because I knew the children were in good hands at home.

The kids, however, were not always as happy with this arrangement. After one of my "visits" to the hospital, I arrived home to a family whose appreciation of me had reached new heights.

Seven year-old Angela greeted me with, "Are we ever glad you're home!"

"You missed me that much?"

"Oh, it wasn't that, Mom. Dad made us eat pink porridge!"

"Pink porridge?" I asked in surprise.

"Yeah, he made the porridge pink. And when we didn't want to eat it, he told us that lots of kids in the world were starving and would be glad to get it." She paused before adding, "Well . . . they could have had mine. It was horrible!"

Apparently, knowing they weren't too fond of porridge, their father thought he'd add some food colouring to make it more appealing to the eye.

I was thinking about that during that last baby drive to the hospital, and smiled to myself. I wondered what he'd think of this time.

When I arrived on the maternity floor, events followed the usual format. I was prepped for delivery, but then the contractions stopped as suddenly as they'd begun. Since it was already two days past my due date, the doctor thought it best that I remain at the hospital. He prescribed a mild sedative, and I was assigned a bed in the labour room. I believe there is a different name for it now, but back then it was called exactly what it sounds like. After all, once you were in there, labour was what you got. Hard labour.

The doctor smiled reassuringly and patted my hand. "Get a good nights' rest and I'll be back in the morning."

Early the following day I was wakened by the onset of labour pains once again, which continued through until late afternoon. I wasn't getting anywhere, but this, too, was normal for me. It was a family joke that it always took me two days to have a baby.

"I think we'll try and speed thing up a little bit," the doctor finally told me. "I'm sure you're as anxious to get this over with as I am."

I was wheeled into the delivery room, where labour was induced, and that suited me fine. I was, indeed, anxious to bring my baby into the world, and I told myself this would be our last child. I had done my share, and found it difficult enough as it was to manage the housework and nine children.

Once real labour began, I wondered why no anesthetic was given to me, but decided it was because the doctor thought it wasn't really necessary. The delivery itself was not particularly difficult, and a few minutes later, my physician exclaimed, "It's a boy!"

"That's nice," I answered, "Now it's even. Five sons, five daughters," and then added, "But he's not crying very much."

I turned slowly in the bed until the baby came into view as he was being cleaned by the nurse on the table, but all I could see was the top of his head. The only sound was his weak baby cry. No one was talking or laughing as they usually do after a normal, healthy birth. But I felt too tired to think much of it at the time. The baby was taken to the nursery shortly afterward, and I was wheeled to my room.

I was eagerly awaiting the arrival of my son at feeding time the following morning, and began thinking of a suitable name. We had nearly run out of ideas.

The woman in the bed beside mine was already nursing her baby, and I noted her happy smile. I knew exactly how she felt.

Lost in thought, I looked up toward the doorway when a voice chimed out, "Good morning, Mrs. Wilkinson. How do you feel?"

It was my pediatrician, and my first impression was that he didn't seem to be in as jovial a mood as usual, but I knew how busy he was.

"I'm fine, thanks, but very anxious to see my baby. Is he on the way in?"

"The nurse will be bringing him shortly, but we have to talk first. There's a problem in the nursery."

"What sort of problem?" I asked, seized by foreboding. I was not prepared for the words that followed.

"Edna. Your baby has all the characteristics of a mongoloid."

I stared back at him, unbelieving, and everything stood still for what seemed like an eternity. My heart. My mind. My world. Time itself.

The word "mongoloid" conjured up a vision of something horrible. I was shocked and stunned. What was a mongoloid? Was my child deformed, disfigured, or some kind of monster? The word had an ugly sound.

The doctor continued talking, but his words came to me from a great distance. It was as if I was standing outside my life, looking on as some other person, a stranger, was being given this terrible news. I tried to speak, but no words came. Numb with disbelief, shock and horror, I could only hear that word "mongoloid" echo in my mind like a needle stuck in a record groove. Mongoloid, mongoloid, mongoloid.

As I lay there thinking this must be a terrible nightmare, I wished I could have died. The woman in the other bed was gazing across at me with pity in her eyes, and I turned my back to her and cried. I scarcely heard the doctor saying, "We'll talk later", as he left the room.

The tears wouldn't stop. Surely it must be my fault, I told myself, or some terrible punishment God was inflicting on me for reasons known only to him. I must have done something wrong. Things like this only happened to other people.

What would I tell my husband, my family and friends? What had I done to deserve something like this? How could I cope with it? Why me, God?

What was I going to do? And in between the questions, I cried. I couldn't tell anyone. I'd never be able to say that word.

When they finally brought the baby in, I was afraid to look at him. I had no idea what to expect, so I just held him in my arms for a while, sitting up in bed, rocking slowly back and forth. The warm little body nestled into me felt like a baby, and smelled like a baby. How bad could it be? And as the tears began to fall again, I told myself that whatever he was, he was mine.

It took all of the courage I could muster to lift the corner of the blanket. I was surprised that he looked almost the same as my other children, and the same feelings of love and tenderness began to flow toward this small bundle of humanity to whom I had given life.

There was the stirring of another emotion, too. A fierce protectiveness welled up inside me, and as I turned, half-defiantly, to the woman in the other bed, she smiled and remarked, "Look at his cute little nose!"

I blessed her silently as I returned her smile. At that moment, an Emily Dickinson line came to mind; "Hope is the thing with feathers that perches in the soul."

I was feeling something inside. Could it, indeed, be hope? Perhaps the doctor was mistaken. Perhaps the baby wasn't a mongoloid. He couldn't be!

However, after the babies were taken back to the nursery, the tears came again. Common sense told me that the pediatrician must be very sure of his diagnosis. He was, after all, a specialist in the field.

As the tears continued to fall, some were for me, and some were for my baby. I wondered if he would ever run and play, or even walk. Would he have anything resembling a normal life?

My mind drifted back to my early teen years, and a young man I often saw on the street. He walked with a shuffling motion, always leaning on a wheelchair, which he usually pushed in front of him. He had little control of his head, as it constantly moved from one side to the other, his mouth hanging open. He often made unintelligible sounds, and everyone said he was "crazy". In my youthful ignorance, I always crossed to the other side of the street when I saw him coming. Would my son endure such a life?

The pediatrician talked with me again the following day, but only succeeded in making me feel worse, if that was possible. He described the condition known as Down's Syndrome, the general expectations and limitations. There would be joys and there would be sorrows.

"You'll have to accept him for what he is," I was told, "He'll need a lot of love and care."

"I don't know how I'll ever be able to accept something like this," I said tearfully.

"You will accept it," he answered gently; "You'll accept it because you have to. There are institutions, and you may want to explore that possibility."

And the thing with feathers flew away, without a backward glance.

Chapter 2

In The Beginning

After giving birth to Christopher Todd, who quickly became simply "Todd" to all who loved him, my emotions progressed from shock, disbelief and sorrow, to resentment and anger. If this had happened because of my age, the doctor must have known that my baby might not be normal. Why hadn't he warned me? Why hadn't I ever heard of such a thing?

I had never before been in close contact with the mentally handicapped. And I never thought it could happen to me. My other nine children were all healthy, and nothing like this had ever been heard of in either my husband's family or mine. What did I know about caring for such a baby? There was nobody to talk to, nobody to advise me. I felt as though I was the only new mother going through this. I felt so alone.

When Todd was five days old, we took him home, and I was despondent.

"What's the use?" I asked myself. "He'll probably never be able to do anything. He'll eat and sleep, cry and fuss, and lie there waiting to be taken care of."

"He'll be all right," Frank said. How could he possibly think everything would be all right?

I had asked the doctor if there was any special care Todd would require. I was told, "Treat him the same as your other children. Love him and enjoy him while you can." I was afraid to ask what that meant.

When we arrived home, I didn't know how to break the news to the other children. I was sure they could never understand. How could I explain it to them when I didn't really understand it myself?

When they realized their baby brother had been born on April first, they laughed and said, "Todd's an April Fool, isn't he, Mom?" And I cried again.

I did more crying than anything else those first few weeks. Remembering the advice to enjoy my baby, I wondered how I was supposed to do that. I thought of the future and wondered what it would bring, for in nineteen sixty-eight, the future for the handicapped was even more uncertain than it is today. I wondered, sometimes, if it was my fault, if there was something wrong with me.

I guess I did my own crying and the baby's too, for he was not at all cross. If he had cried at night like the other children had, it would have been more encouraging. Oh, I felt sorry for myself.

I endured long, silent conversations with God, in which I alternately prayed, questioned, pleaded, raged and rebelled. It wasn't fair, and I just couldn't handle it. Why did He let such things happen?

When my emotions were finally spent, I listened, as though a loud, thunderous voice from the heavens would reply with explicit instructions about what to do. There was nothing but silence, and I thought, "There's no help anywhere. There's only me. And I don't know where to go from here."

The days followed one another in an endless routine of bathing, feeding, changing dirty diapers, and caring for the other children, as well. Some were in school, and some were still at home. Cooking and cleaning often took second place to all the other demands on my time, and always, in the back of my mind, was the sadness, resentment, and worry about my Down's baby. I needed to obtain more information and advice, but I had no idea where to start.

By the time Todd's six week check-up with the pediatrician rolled around, my state of mind hadn't changed much. I was operating solely on instinct where my baby was concerned, and was hoping the doctor would give me a more encouraging report.

After the usual weight and height check, the physician said that everything seemed to be going well. Still thinking that my situation was an isolated case, I wondered aloud how many Down's babies he'd seen. His answer surprised me.

"I know of one very special Down's child," he replied with a smile. "She was my daughter, and she brought more joy to our family than any normal child could have. We had her with us for nineteen years."

Noting he used the word "had", I asked, "Where is she now?"

"She had a serious heart condition," he answered sadly. "We decided to go ahead with surgery to correct it, but she died during the operation."

"I'm sorry," seemed an inadequate reply, but I didn't know what else to say. I suddenly saw him in a completely different light. Instead of being merely a doctor, he was a friend, and suddenly I had found a kindred spirit, of sorts. He probably had experienced many of the same feelings I had at some point, but had known much more sorrow. I was a little ashamed at feeling so sorry for myself, and I no longer felt quite so alone.

"But", he continued, "This little fellow is in pretty good shape. He does have a slight heart murmur, but nothing to worry about at this point. It is possible he will outgrow it."

The thing with feathers fluttered briefly in my heart again.

"Of course," he continued, "There will be many changes as Todd grows older, some of them better than others. Take each day as it comes, and follow your instincts."

"But what if I do something wrong?" I queried nervously. "I don't know how to raise a mentally handicapped baby."

He smiled reassuringly. "You've had nine other babies. This one is no different, really. He needs the same things for now. Love and care."

There was that suggestion again, this "for now" business. The same thing I'd heard in the hospital when they said, "Enjoy him while you can."

The doctor's parting words were, "Relax, don't worry so much, and if you run into any problems, I'm as close as the telephone."

I wasn't sure about relaxing, but I was sure he'd be getting more than his share of calls.

Chapter 3

The Early Years

Life at home became almost normal, apart from my continuing depression over what seemed to be an insurmountable problem. I tried, gradually, to make the other children aware that Todd was a little different from them. It's difficult to explain something like Down's Syndrome to children in a language they will understand, when you scarcely understand it yourself. It didn't appear to change their feelings for him, though, so I took the same course of action with family and friends. After the initial shock had passed, everyone was very supportive and understanding.

For a long time I was embarrassed to take Todd along on outings because I imagined everyone would stare at him. I guess I had my own kind of prejudice, and there was still the feeling that people would blame me and think it was my fault in some way. There were stares as he got a little older, but I tried not to notice, even though it was difficult to ignore the bewildered glances that began when we came into view, and followed us until we disappeared out of sight.

At home, there was less need for me to be on the defensive, and it soon became easier to relax a little more. We began including Todd in our home movies, and the first time he stood up alone, even though he wobbled unsteadily back and forth, was duly recorded on camera. The entire family witnessed the great event, and there was much applauding. Seeing this, Todd smiled happily and clapped his hands together, too.

At about a year and a half, he began to walk, despite my earlier fears. His speech, however, did not develop nearly as well. He knew how to get what he wanted, though. With everyone in the family at his beck and call, he had only to point to something, and it was in his hands. I realize now that it was the wrong thing to do, but at the time there were no experts available. There was only his family, who loved him.

At times he was very independent, and when he first insisted on feeding himself, it was bedlam. He'd grab the food in his chubby fingers and aim it in the general direction of his mouth. Then the fingers would open to smear their contents over his entire face and head. Or, he'd wave the dish aloft and set it neatly atop his head, as the food slid or plopped (according to its consistency), all over his body. I soon became a little wiser, and covered the floor beneath his high chair with newspapers.

No matter how messy he was, though, his impish smile beamed through it all, and I was caught up in his spell.

About this time, we had the opportunity to purchase an old farmhouse in the country, thirty miles away. Todd figured prominently in our decision. We decided it would be ideal for him, with lots of fresh, country air, and thirty acres of land where he could roam and play. We had no way of knowing that the day would come when we would wish for a little less roaming space.

Of course, I have to admit that I was eager to buy the place for my own reasons. It happened to be the house where I had spent my childhood, and it held many happy memories for me. So we bought the house and moved in one hot, August day. And a new way of life began for all of us.

Chapter 4

Life In The Country

For weeks I had regaled my family with tales of my happy childhood. What it had been like to roam the countryside, carefree and content. How the birds woke you on summer mornings with their melodious call, and how milk straight from the cow to the table was sweeter than nectar. Winter was a dream come true, I told them, with beautiful, crisp, white snow underfoot, not to mention the smell of wood smoke hanging on the frosty air. And of course, they'd be ecstatic with a country Christmas! We'd cut our own tree, carry it home through the fields, and decorate it on Christmas Eve while we sang Christmas carols.

That first day when we drove into the yard, all we could see was tall weeds and long grass.

"Wow," one of the boys exclaimed, "The grass sure grows high out here."

"Won't take long to get ride of that," Frank answered. The look he sent my way, however, said, "This is what you call carefree and content?"

"Come on," I said, "Let's fix a snack. Things will look different in the morning."

And they did! Everything looked older and smaller than I remembered. Todd kept getting lost in the tall grass; and he'd stand still and scream until someone rescued him.

When we tried to buy some of that nice, fresh milk from a neighboring farmer, we were reminded of quotas, and the fact that fresh milk wasn't considered to be as healthy these days. I could see that things in the country had changed, and I was disappointed.

By the time summer was over, things were more or less in shape, and before we knew it, Christmas arrived. On Christmas Eve there was a steady fall of snow, and the countryside looked beautiful.

"Well, Mom," I was reminded, "At least you were right about the snow. I hate to think how deep it's going to be in the morning, though!"

It was a cold winter, but we managed to keep warm and busy. Each day was a new experience for all of us. The children were settled in school, and Todd and I were alone through the day.

When the first days of spring settled over the land, it was beautiful. Todd thought so too, and wanted to spend most of his time outdoors.

He was nearly four years old now, and a bundle of dynamite in motion. Our house was very close to the highway, and directly behind the house was a creek that flowed into a bay. We couldn't let Todd out of sight, for he had no fear of anything, except long grass, and being underneath trees.

We installed large hooks at the tops of all the doors that led outside, but he still managed to dart past anyone going in or out, and in a flash he'd be gone.

Whereas some Down's children are very calm and passive, Todd was exactly the opposite. He moved with lightning speed as he ran from room to room, leaving a path of destruction in his wake, overturning chairs, shredding paper, and strewing clothing about. He'd spill things, throw objects thorough the air, and make the worst messes imaginable. On one occasion, he climbed up on the kitchen cabinet and poured salt and pepper into the sugar bowl. I found out about that when I took a nice big sip of coffee.

It was the same thing upstairs. It was difficult to understand how he managed to propel himself so swiftly up and down the steep steps without breaking some bones in a fall. I finally came to the conclusion that his life was charmed, and that God looks out for His own.

The bedroom doors had hooks, too, but if someone neglected to fasten them, it made Todd's day. He emptied dresser drawers, and stripped beds down to the mattresses. His sisters' liquid makeup was mixed with perfume and cologne, and poured over dressers and dressing tables. All this could be accomplished in a matter of minutes. When the potent aroma began wafting through the house, we knew exactly where it originated from. His favourite type of artistry was scribbling on mirrors with lipstick.

The older children were, understandably, often frustrated and upset, but no more than I was, and I began to go on the defensive.

"What do you want me to do?" I'd scream, "I'll clean up the mess, I'll buy more makeup, and make the beds!"

"Oh, Mom, don't be silly. It's not your fault. You don't have to buy more makeup. "You'd never be able to afford it, anyway."

But I felt it was my fault, and I felt guilty because I didn't know how to cope with these incidents, or how to discipline Todd. Punishment had no effect, and he rarely cried. He would only become more stubborn and angry, shouting, "No, no!" over and over. And half an hour later, he'd be doing something even worse.

At times, I was sure I was losing my mind. I couldn't sit down for five minutes, and by the end of the day, I was exhausted. Todd never seemed to get tired, and I was sure I covered a hundred miles a day just trying to keep up with him.

I was constantly in a state of anxiety worrying that visitors might drop in while the house was in a state of disarray. They often did, and then it was a case of run and grab what you could, and toss it into the nearest cupboard or corner before the door opened. As the knocking grew more persistent, I'd hear one of the kids yell, "Can I open it yet?"

This little whirlwind with feet soon figured some things out. He was using the thinking process, that's for sure, and if he had used all that energy in the opposite direction from what he was doing, he could have moved all the mountains that stood in his way.

He discovered that, by using a broom handle or some other long object, he could easily push up the hooks on the doors. In a flash, he'd be outside, running down the line in the centre of the road, with me in hot pursuit. It did no good to call or threaten him. He only ran faster, laughing with glee because this was a very good game, and he had someone to join in with him.

Having twisted my ankle once during this game, I began to think like him. In the warm weather, it did seem easier to run without shoes, so I followed his example. My weight stayed even at one hundred and ten pounds with no need to diet. The neighbours had a lot of free shows, and they were doubtless awestruck at times by the sight of the two of us barreling down the centre of the road, with me always bringing up the rear in my bare feet.

The most difficult part was getting him back to the house after the capture. He was usually carried home, kicking and screaming all the way.

Our big barn was another trouble spot. Todd liked nothing better than to hide there, and climb the built-in ladder that led up to the big hayloft overhead. If he wasn't caught by the time he reached the first rung of that ladder, it meant trouble. If he made it to the top, there was a chance he might fall through an opening between the floor boards.

Whoever happened to be the pursuer had to climb the ladder behind him, catch him in their arms, and navigate the tricky descent back down to the bottom, with a kicking, screaming bundle as their cargo. Day after day there were new problems to overcome. I had nightmares in which he escaped outdoors while we were all sleeping, and disappeared forever.

There were humorous incidents, too. Times when I laughed just for the good feeling it gave me. Like the time we had the setting hen who developed the habit of leaving her nest of eggs every so often to roam the yard, invading my flower beds, and scratching out all the flower seeds which I had so painstakingly planted. I complained about her constantly, and chased her back to the barn several times a day. Needless to say, Todd loved giving a helping hand with this activity.

One day, there was a great commotion out in the yard. I heard cackling, squawking, and screams of delight. Running to investigate, I found the poor hen dashing madly around in circles, with water dripping from her bedraggled feathers, while her eggs went untended in the nest.

Todd was still holding the empty pail, but I didn't have the inclination or the heart to chastise him. I laughed until my sides hurt, feeling a certain satisfaction at the sight of the cringing hen. It seemed like perfect justice to me.

I wondered if this was the sort of enjoyment the doctor had meant. I didn't think so, but it was a good feeling to laugh again. The hen was no worse for the experience, but she did stay closer to her nest after that. Eventually, she hatched seven fluffy yellow chicks, and they all lived happily ever after.

I don't know how I would have managed without the other children. The two eldest girls, Angela and Maureen, were married and living in their own homes, so they were slightly removed from the chaos. However, when they came to visit, as they often did, they were apt to find themselves caught up in the tangled web of our upside-down life.

Those still living at home, however, were my lifeline to sanity. Debby, Heather, Becky, Joe, Terry, Ken and Dave were seven extra pairs of eyes and hands. I'd like to be able to say that none of their wants and needs were ever neglected because of my preoccupation with Todd, but I know that's exactly what happened on occasion. Their complaints were few, but I guess they had good reason to resent Todd at times, and me as well.

I began to dread the sound of their footsteps going up the stairs. There would be silence for a minute or so, and then a voice would yell, "Mom, Todd's been in my room again!"

"Oh, no. How bad is it this time?"

"Well, you'd better come and look. He's got all the blankets off the bed and right now he's jumping on the mattress!"

So we'd try to get Todd to help with the clean-up, but that wasn't his style. He was always happiest in the midst of the debris.

Still, the others were always on the look-out for him, and if he was outside, that was even more important. I'd step outdoors for a breath of fresh air on a warm summer evening, and as soon as I appeared in sight, one of them would call, "He's over here, Mom!" Of course, we all knew who "he" was.

Or, I'd be working in the kitchen and see something flash by the window. Running to the door, I'd hear, "I've got him, Mom. He's taking his clothes off again and there's a car coming!"

Modesty was not one of Todd's strong points, and he had no compunction about stripping if he felt like it. One day he went outdoors with pants on and came back in without them. I have a feeling they ended up in the marsh behind the barn.

There were times when various articles were misplaced or lost, and Todd often took the blame for it, whether he was guilty or not. Unable to speak plainly enough to be understood, he couldn't tell us if he was responsible. When asked if he knew where the missing object was, he'd nod his head, and then proceed to lead us on a wild goose chase. We usually ended up finding nothing.

We once searched for a set of car keys for an entire Saturday afternoon on the chance that they were in the back yard where Todd said they were. The "lost keys" turned up later. Much later. They'd been hanging on a hook in the kitchen all along, but nobody thought to look there. Everyone felt terrible afterward because Todd had been wrongfully accused.

He did like keys, though, and cars, too. He enjoyed climbing into them and pretending he was driving. One night after supper he went outdoors while the rest of the family was still at the table. Someone glanced out the window and screamed, "There goes the car, and Todd's in it!"

Sure enough, the car was moving slowly past the kitchen window, and all that was visible in the driver's seat was Todd's head, with one of my dish towels draped over it. Frank and Joe made a dash for the door and "he" was rescued before any harm came to car or driver. After it was over we were able to laugh about it, but at the time it was very frightening. We made a pact that from then on, everyone would remove their car keys when they left the vehicle, even if it was for only a few minutes.

This brings to mind the incident of a man and his canoe. He came to the door one day in late spring to ask if he could put his canoe in the water behind the house.

"Of course," I told him, "Just be sure you lock your car and take the keys with you."

When he asked why, I told him about Todd, and that he liked to climb in cars to play. When I mentioned the words "mentally handicapped", it was as if I had said that a ferocious dog was ready to attack.

Without another word, he backed out the door, got into his car, and drove quickly away. I really had a laugh about that.

There is a low bridge a short distance from our house where people sometimes come to fish in the warm weather, and Todd was often known to run over there to see what was going on.

The fishers sit on the bridge with their legs hanging over the side, and their backs to the road.

One Sunday afternoon, we noticed Todd heading in that direction, and by the time Debby reached him, he was busily occupied filling someone's tackle box with gravel from the side of the road. Understandably, the fisherman was not pleased.

On another occasion, we were visiting Maureen in Kingston. As it was a warm summer day, we decided to sit outside. I wasn't too sure about this arrangement because I knew how closely we would have to watch Todd. However, Maureen volunteered to oversee him, so I wasn't paying too much attention until he suddenly dropped his toys and ran for the street.

Maureen immediately ran after him, but he was already halfway down the block. Just before she caught up with him, he disappeared through someone's front door, and when she got inside, he was running around the dining room table, screaming with laughter, as the lady of the house stood watching in shocked amazement. All Maureen could do was apologize and grab Todd, leaving the lady speechless.

There were moments when I fantasized how it would be if he couldn't walk for twenty-four hours, and felt like a monster afterward. It would be so good to keep him in one spot, just for a day. I was prone to momentary lapses such as this when things got out of hand.

On one occasion, I thought his legs were gone, maybe his entire body. We'd been having some very mild spring weather, and our garden was a sea of mud. Late one afternoon as I was preparing supper, I saw Becky run screaming toward the house.

"Mom, come quick! Todd's stuck in the mud!"

"I'm coming. Where is he?"

"In the garden. Hurry up, he's sinking right down in the mud!"

I grabbed a thick pair of men's socks and a pair of big rubber boots. Pulling them on quickly, I ran as fast as they would allow in the direction of Todd's calls for help, with Becky close behind me.

"Hep me, hep me," (help me), I heard.

"O.k., stand still, and don't try to move!" I was glad I'd had all that prior experience in running.

As soon as I saw him, I could tell there was no need to caution him against moving about. I wasn't more than three feet into the garden before I, too, was mired down. As I tried to lift my feet, off came first one boot, and then the other. The socks didn't last much longer, and soon they, too, were buried in the mud. It was like quicksand! Out of the corner of my eye I saw Becky's running shoes disappear from sight.

She made it to Todd before I did. My feet were freezing, and as I staggered along I was mumbling words under my breath that I won't repeat. We both pulled as hard as we could, but couldn't budge him. The mud was up to his knees, and we were becoming desperate. When he sank still lower, I knew we had to do something quickly.

"Come on," I said, "We'll have to pull him out of his boots!"

So that's what we did. And between the two of us, we carried him back to the house, all of us in our bare feet, and covered in mud. Somewhere, at the bottom of that garden, are two pairs of boots, various socks, one pair of running shoes, and a lot of cuss words. However, none of us were any worse for the experience so, as they say, all's well that ends well.

Todd and I were still having our road races, and I decided it was time to look for a solution. I enlisted the help of a counselor who came to the house once a week to work on the problem.

She suggested confining him to his room for half an hour each time he went on the road, and added that I should explain to him why it was being done. At first it was very difficult. He'd cry and yell, "'et me out!", over and over. However, within three weeks he was beginning to get the idea, and in about a month and a half, the problem was solved. From then on his energy was expended in the house and surrounding area.

Chapter 5

School Begins

Although Todd had now reached the age of five years, toilet training had been impossible up to this point. No matter how I tried, there was very little progress. And just when we seemed to be gaining ground, he would go upstairs, or in the living room, and make a mess on the floor. While I was busy cleaning that up, he'd be in the kitchen emptying the cupboards. It was like playing ring around the rosy, with me, of course, being the rosy.

At my wits' end, I didn't know what to try next. One minute I felt optimistic over some small accomplishment, and the next minute, a great wave of depression would sweep over me when a failure loomed like a mighty mountain. When all efforts failed, there were conversations with God again. Either He wasn't hearing me too well, or the absence of any hoped-for miracle meant that He was trying to tell me it was my problem and I'd have to handle it.

I had never imagined in my wildest dreams that Todd would ever be able to attend school. However one day, while having a conversation with a neighbour, she mentioned that there was a school for the mentally handicapped in the area, and I contacted the principal to find out if there was any chance that Todd might be accepted there.

She was very receptive, and set up an interview at home to meet us. A member of the Board of Education came with her, and unfortunately, Todd was at his worst that day, jumping and climbing over furniture. Then he'd scoot into the next room, and there'd be a loud crash as something was knocked over, followed by the sound of his mischievous laugh.

I answered their questions as best I could, but embarrassment overcame me. I was sure everything was lost, for it was unbelievable that any school would accept such a child. After about an hour the principal left, promising to contact me when a decision was reached by the Board. I wasn't holding my breath waiting.

So I was very surprised when I received word a week later that Todd would be accepted at Morven School as soon as he was fully toilet trained. My spirits soared momentarily, but there was a lot of work ahead. So . . . back to the bathroom!

The struggle continued, but Todd scored more points than me. He was a good size now, and if he decided he wasn't going to sit on the toilet, his entire body went limp and floppy as he slid down onto the floor, repeating the word that he could say most clearly and emphatically, "No, no, no!" When I was able to coax him to climb back on, he'd sit for ten minutes with no result, and as soon as he was dressed again, there'd be another mess to clean up.

Then God took pity on me, I guess, for there came what seemed to be the answer to some of my prayers. He had probably been hearing me, all right, and was tired of listening to my whining.

I happened to run into a childhood friend who was now assistant supervisor of a children's ward at a psychiatric hospital in Kingston. She suggested that it might be a good idea to enroll Todd in a training program at the hospital, as toilet training was one of the areas they dealt with. If I was interested, I could contact the hospital. If I was interested?!?! Could a bird fly? I was on the telephone to the hospital within the hour. It sounded like exactly what Todd needed, but there was one big problem. He would have to be admitted to the institution for at least a three week period, perhaps longer. The length of time he spent there would depend on how well he did with the toilet training.

Even though life with him was hectic, I wasn't sure if I was prepared to let him go away for such a length of time. It would be his first time away from home by himself. Some of the family thought it would be cruel to put him in "that place", and this made my decision more difficult than ever.

After much discussion, we all agreed that toilet training was in Todd's best interest, and we went ahead with the arrangements.

You never saw so many long faces as the day we drove him to the hospital. I was almost in tears myself, and had to keep reminding myself that it had to be done. It almost broke my heart to leave him there among strangers and walk away. It was as if part of me was left behind in that austere building with doors that were always locked. All the way home, I felt as if someone had died.

In fact, the house was quiet as a tomb without Todd. I had promised myself that I would keep busy by getting caught up on all the chores that were neglected when he was around, but I couldn't settle down to anything. I didn't know what to do with myself. Suddenly, there were so many hours in which to do as I pleased, and there didn't seem to be any way to fill them. At night, I imagined I heard his voice calling from far off in the distance, and I'd rouse from sleep, wondering if he was all right.

We were told it would be better if we didn't visit him for a couple of days so that he would have the opportunity to become accustomed to the new surroundings. Well, that was as much time as I could wait without knowing what was going on.

I'm sure our family must have greatly annoyed the staff of Ward One, dropping in almost every day to check on Todd's progress. But we were always made to feel welcome by the counselors and staff, and they were happy to explain the methods they were using. He was wakened at regular intervals throughout the night to use the bathroom, and their methods were working much better than mine had. At home, I was just too exhausted at night to wake him every hour.

Through the day there was lots of playtime, inside and out, and also music classes, which Todd was very happy with. He was enjoying all the attention he was getting, and seemed to be adapting well, but always wanted to come home with us when we left. I was glad this wasn't a permanent arrangement, because I could never have endured so many tearful farewells.

He got along very well with most of the other children there, with the exception of one little girl, who was autistic. Since she was unable to speak, most of her communicating was done through screaming.

There were many toys in the playroom for the children, and one was a special favourite of both Todd and the little girl, whom I shall call Mary. (Not her real name.) Often, they both insisted on riding the spring rocking horse at the same time.

Mary would climb on the horse, and that was Todd's cue to try and force her to dismount. One day, as I watched in dismay, and before either I or one of the counselors could move to stop him, he descended on Mary in a frenzy, wrapped his fingers in her hair, and shouted, "bong gong!", while trying to pull her from the horse's back. Screaming shrilly, she climbed down, and a victorious Todd was soon sitting astride the mount.

We never discovered where he heard that expression, or what it meant, but from that day on, it became his battle cry. Whenever we heard the dreaded, "bong gong", we knew it meant trouble for someone or some thing.

Todd needed extensive dental work, and since he had to be treated while under anesthetic, it meant he had to be transferred to that section of the hospital where surgery was performed. Down's children often have a history of poor dental health, and Todd required seven extractions, among other things.

The nurses were kept busy supervising his antics while he was waiting to be treated. Often they'd put him in a laundry cart and push him around the halls as they performed their duties, which suited him just fine.

If he sometimes broke free, he harassed the adult male patients unmercifully. When he saw them go into the bathroom, he'd follow them in, get down on his stomach on the floor, and peek under the cubicle to see who was in there. When they shouted at him, he'd scramble out backwards, laughing with glee. The older patients were more sober, and Todd was a little too vocal for their liking. I did feel rather indebted to an adult Down's patient in his early forties who took Todd under his wing, so to speak.

"I look affer 'im," he told me, "I like 'im, he my 'ittle boy."

Strangely, I was quite confident that my son would, indeed, be cared for by this man if any of the other patients became upset.

Finally, the day arrived for Todd's dental work to be done, and when it was over, I felt terrible when I first caught sight of him. I still recall the mournful expression in his eyes as he gazed at me, hazy from the anesthetic. His mouth had been bleeding from the extractions, and tiny streaks of blood were running down his chin, some of it dried. I had never seen him look so forlorn. I wanted to stay and hold him, but it was time to leave, and the nurse said he would probably sleep for the next few hours. So all I could do was kiss him and tell him that I would be back. It was some consolation to know that he would soon be coming home.

The toilet training turned out to be a huge success, thanks to the well-trained and dedicated staff at the hospital. Todd came home six weeks after he began the program, and a few months later, he started classes at Morven School, near Napanee, Ontario.

And This Is Love

He kisses my hand, and he brushes my face
With fingers as soft as the touch of spun lace;
And his bright eyes of blue, filled with mischief and glee
Turn my world upside down when he smiles at me.
Then he runs, and I follow, to heaven knows where,
This small streak of lightning with never a care;
He's a mischief, a worry, a whirlwind with feet,
But without him around, life is just not complete.
He scribbles with crayons on windows and doors,
For paper, to him, is for spreading on floors;
He empties my cupboards of kettles and things,
But when he says, "Hi, Mom," oh how my heart sings!
He may never be brilliant, or worldly, or wise,
But there's happiness, laughter and love in his eyes;
And no matter how many faults others may see,
He is happiness, laughter, and great love to me.

Edna M. Wilkinson

Chapter 6

More Steps Up The Mountain

School was a definite turning point for Todd, and for me it was heaven. There were now six full hours each day when I didn't have to be looking over my shoulder every minute, or have eyes in the back of my head. There were still problems, but at least there was some relief.

The teachers were wonderfully caring, and it was a new experience for me to have someone who understood the problems I faced; to know people who could advise and sympathize. The realization that there were other people with problems similar to mine bolstered my spirits immensely. There were school activities where I met other parents with like interests, and it was most helpful to discuss and compare our problems. I was not alone any more.

There were school concerts, bus trips, and other social events for the students, and parents were usually invited to participate. There were shopping trips at Christmas time when the students drew names for gift giving. Of course, there was always time to pay a visit to Santa Claus. On one visit, Todd tried to pull Santa's beard off, and the "Ho, ho, ho" sounded much more like, "No, no no!"

Morven students participated, once a year, in special church services throughout the area. Their choir did well, and was always given a warm welcome wherever they performed. It was a moving experience to listen as they sang "We Shall Overcome", "He's Got The Whole World In His Hands", and "Everything Is Beautiful". Even Todd was included, for some sang well and compensated for those with speech problems. A few joys were finally moving in to take away some of the sorrow, and I was ready to welcome them with open arms.

However, even though we had taken a few small steps forward, there was always another problem waiting in the wings. Todd seemed to be enjoying school, but sometimes decided he would rather stay home and play, and changing his mind was often an exercise in futility. On these occasions, when it was time to get dressed, he'd throw himself on the floor, his body going limp. Moaning, "I tick, I tick," (sick), and rubbing his stomach, he'd writhe in apparent agony. He was very convincing at times, causing me to believe that he really was in genuine pain, but most of the time, I knew it was just a ploy to get his own way.

When I refused to give in to his pleas, things turned into a regular circus. He became bad-tempered and rebellious, glaring at me defiantly, as if daring me to touch him. If I attempted to pull his pants on, he pushed them down, stubbornly refusing to cooperate in any way. When dressing was finally accomplished, the worst was yet to come.

Pushing, pulling, half dragging and half carrying, trying not to let my temper get the best of me, we'd finally make it out to the road to wait for the bus. Once it arrived, he'd see the other children and climb aboard with no more objections. Afterward, I'd go thankfully inside, collapse breathlessly into the nearest chair, and sit for thirty minutes or so, enjoying the heavenly peace and quiet.

One day while we were waiting for the bus, he ran outside and locked himself in a car that was parked in the driveway. The keys weren't around to unlock it, and he refused to open the door from the inside, despite all my pleading and threatening. The bus arrived in the middle of the stand-off, and I didn't know what to do. One of the older boys on the bus got out and walked over to the car.

"Come on, Todd," he said. "Come on, let's go to school."

Without another word, Todd unlocked the door and climbed out of the car and onto the bus, leaving me standing in the middle of the driveway feeling very inadequate.

When I did give him the benefit of the doubt and allowed him to stay at home, nothing could hold him down once the bus had left. One warm day in early June, he had pulled the "at death's door" routine, and I didn't have the stomach for a fight that morning. I thought, "Oh well, maybe it will be different today."

"No shenanigans," I warned him, "Be a good boy, or you'll have to stay in your room all day!"

He played quietly for a few minutes, sitting on the floor idly flipping through the pages of a picture book. He often did that, sitting with legs outstretched, book on his lap. He'd hold the pages in one hand, staring intently as the colorful pictures flipped quickly past his face. I decided it was safe to turn my back long enough to wash the breakfast dishes. Wrong decision! When I turned around a minute later, he was gone.

Debby had a little brown puppy named Cocoa, which had been a gift from her Uncle Jim. Todd loved to race around the yard with Cocoa at his heels, laughing with delight as she nipped at his feet. On this particular morning, I stepped outside to see where he had disappeared to this time, and I immediately heard yelps and squeals, mingled with Todd's shouts of glee. Thinking they were enjoying one of their romps, I walked toward the back of the house where the commotion seemed to be coming from.

As I rounded the corner, I could see Todd jumping up and down, his eyes glued in fascination on a large rain barrel which I knew was full of water. Running to the barrel, I soon found the source of the yelps. He had thrown Cocoa into the water, and she was paddling frantically, desperately trying to keep her head above water.

Grabbing her up quickly, I dashed into the house, wrapped her small, shivering body in a large bath towel, and laid her on the couch. For hours afterward she shivered and shook, faint sob-like yelps breaking the silence.

Todd did get a spanking for that episode, but it hurt his pride more than anything else. A few minutes later he was busily occupied burying a box of his father's roofing nails in the sand pile. Which, by the way, were retrieved by sifting the entire pile of sand through a piece of window screen. The process took several days and many pairs of hands.

I think he wanted to stay home from school many days so that he could spend more time outdoors, because that's where he most liked to be. At school there was only recess and lunch time to run free, and there was nothing interesting to mess up. On our first interview with his teacher, she complained that it was very difficult to persuade him to go back to his room after the mid-day break.

"I have a terrible time getting him back inside," she told me, "I find him lying on his back on the grass, arms underneath his head, just staring up at the sky."

I couldn't really blame him, for I recalled enjoying many a lazy summer afternoon when I was young, watching the fluffy white cloud patterns as they drifted across the blue heavens. Todd was probably doing the same thing. And I thought how interesting it would be if he could only tell us his thoughts.

The following year, his new teacher was a young woman who had very long, pretty hair, and her locks fascinated Todd so much that he tried to emulate it at home.

Draping a towel or something similar over his head, he'd let it hang down around his shoulders. Then he'd swing his head back and forth, saying that the towel was, "hair". I couldn't see anything really harmful in the habit, thinking he would soon forget about it. However, it continued over a long period of time, and if the towel was taken away, he soon found another one.

"He's using it as a kind of security blanket," a friend said. "You know, the same way a baby has a special blanket to take everywhere." She had no idea he was pretending it was hair.

Frank had a different view of the whole thing. "Take that thing away from him," he told me, "He'll be running around like that for the rest of his life if you let him!"

Eventually, the phase passed, and we all breathed a sigh of relief. What would the next fad be?

Each time any of the students at Morven accomplished something new, they were given a certificate to bring home. It was a red-letter day when Todd received his first. It read, "Today Todd was chosen Student of the Day at Morven School for swimming with water wings without any support."

He had taken one more step up the mountain.

Time and tide wait for no man, or woman, or child, and while Todd was busy making his mark in the field of learning, his brothers and sisters were not sitting idly by. With all those hours expended in re-making beds, acting as helping hands to me, and part-time babysitters for their younger brother, I'm surprised they found the time or strength to pursue their own interests and inclinations; but family life went on.

Debby was absorbed with her job as Court Clerk in Provincial Court in Napanee. Working five days a week, she nevertheless devoted many of her off-duty hours to the preservation of my sanity, assisting me with numerous household chores, and taking Todd under her wing when necessary. She had long ago forgiven him for Cocoa's dunking.

Joe was working in the fuel oil business and Terry was an auto body repair apprentice. Heather was employed at Millhaven Fibres, while Becky, Dave and Ken were still attending school. Heather, however, was becoming increasingly dissatisfied with her job.

"I want to do something else with my life," she told me. "Maybe some kind of work with children. I don't think I want to spend the rest of my life standing behind a machine."

"Have you got anything in particular in mind?" I asked. I could understand how she felt.

"A friend at work was telling me today there's a course I could take to become a counselor for the mentally handicapped. It would mean going back to school to get my high school diploma, and then I'd have to go to college. But I'd really like to try it."

"I think you should look into, then," I told her. "If you really want to do it, I'm sure you can. You certainly know what you'd be getting into, after all the experience you've had with Todd."

I wondered, silently, if she'd seriously considered what it would be like working closely with a group of such children instead of just one, but I was secretly pleased that she was choosing such a worthwhile goal to pursue. Perhaps there was a slightly selfish motive in my thinking, too. I would, no doubt, benefit from information she'd be able to give me in the course of her studies. Information that would surely help me to cope more intelligently with problems I experienced with Todd. Heaven knows, I needed all the help I could get.

So, the learning process began. The first step was enrolling in classes as St. Lawrence College in Kingston, to work toward her high school diploma. This accomplished, she was well on her way to realize the goal she had set.

Student loans were available, and in September, 1975, Heather was accepted at Loyalist College in Belleville, Ontario. It was a two-year course which proved to be a challenging one, but she progressed well. When she came home on weekends and holidays, she was able to give me many helpful pointers and suggestions.

I discovered, for instance, that for people like Todd, the reward system is most effective. If the child complies with a request to carry out a specific action in a satisfactory manner, he receives something in return. This could be anything from a shopping excursion to a favourite candy or other treat. It should, however, be something the child is particularly fond of. This method often worked with Todd when all else failed, and I was reminded that his should not be thought of as bribery. After all, we all operate on the reward system. We go to work and receive a paycheque, so this is our reward. If we work hard and well, we may get a promotion; so once again, we are compensated for our efforts.

I think the reward system comes under the heading of psychology, and all parents use it from time to time, whether they are aware of it or not. I think we all know that the surest way to persuade a child to do something is to suggest that you don't want him or her to do it. Nine times out of ten, the child is sure to do what you want him to if he thinks you're against it. Sounds complicated, but it seems to be the way human nature works.

I began to enjoy trying out my own psychology. It wasn't always successful, but at least I felt it was something positive. A step in the right direction.

When Todd headed up the stairs, I encouraged him. "I'd like you to go upstairs and play, Todd."

He'd stand quiet still for a few seconds, looking at me with a puzzled expression on his face.

"No!" he'd stubbornly reply, and he'd march back down the steps. Score one for Mom! Well, that was one mess that wouldn't have to be cleaned up by anyone, so I figured the end justified the means.

There was a lot for the entire family to learn. With so many of us around, we had developed the habit of scrambling to give him whatever he wanted, without having to ask for it verbally. We worked on the problem, but old habits die hard.

Todd, meanwhile, was settling down nicely into the school schedule, and there were improvements in certain areas. His behaviour was improving, and he began to look forward to the bus arriving in the driveway every morning. We realized, however, that we could not expect too much academically.

The Rotary Club of Napanee sponsored swimming and bowling lessons weekly for the Morven students. Each Tuesday they made the trip to Kingston by bus, bowling one week, swimming the next. To this day, Tuesday is still Todd's favourite day of the week. In the beginning he was rather timid about being in the pool, but he soon went from sitting on a chair to wearing water wings. Nowadays, swimming is one of his favourite activities, and he is very good at it. In our pool at home, he dives like a dolphin, and when we go to the cottage, it's difficult to get him to leave the water until he is wrinkled like a prune.

Heather successfully completed her course, graduating at the top of her class, a qualified Mental Retardation Counselor, (M.R.C.), and found employment at the Adult Rehabilitation Centre in Kingston.

She says that Todd was largely responsible for her decision to enter the profession so, indirectly, he is helping many others like himself.

A very worthwhile accomplishment for someone who is known as mentally handicapped!

Chapter 7

A Crisis Of A Different Kind

It was a great relief to have Todd settled in school and in a regular routine. I felt as though a heavy weight had been lifted from my shoulders, and I eased into a routine of my own that allowed me to accomplish household chores while he was in class. It also gave me more time to supervise him in the evenings and on weekends, which was when his new schedule gave him free reign to let his energetic creativity run riot.

Then, just when it appeared we had reached a plateau of sorts and were leveling out for a while, some problems of a different nature surfaced.

Ken, who was fifteen and in his second year of high school, began having nosebleeds which gradually became more severe. After he had lost several days of school because of this, we decided it was time to seek medical advice. On the morning that I was about to contact our family doctor to set up an appointment, I heard Ken's voice coming from the living room.

"Mom, come and look at my legs. There are little black spots all over them."

Famous for his clowning around, I thought it was another of Ken's practical jokes.

"Well with my luck," I replied lightly, "I've probably got a kid who's invented a new disease. I wonder if it's contagious. I don't think the spots are really black, but you'd better use your own cup and towel until we find out what it is."

This last remark was meant as a joke, but I thought I'd better have a look anyway.

On going to investigate, it was obvious at once that this was no joke.

The small, dark purplish spots covered his legs as well as other areas of his body. I had never seen anything like it before, and it frightened me. Our doctor set up an appointment for the following day. After examining Ken thoroughly, he appeared worried, too.

"I can't be positive without more tests," he said, "But it looks like a blood disease called Purpura. I'm going to send you to a blood specialist in Kingston."

"How serious is it?" I asked.

"It could be very serious. All you can do for now is keep him as quiet as possible, and don't let him do anything strenuous."

He explained that the purplish spots were caused by small blood vessels under the skin which had ruptured, and any blow or knock to the body could result in more severe bleeding. The term "Purpura" comes from the colour of the spots appearing on the skin.

Two days before the appointment with the specialist, Ken was hit with an attack worse than any of the others had been. He came downstairs holding a blood-stained towel over his nose. It was almost time for Todd's bus, and I didn't know what to do.

"Put your head back," I told Ken, "And try to keep still. As soon as Todd leaves on the bus, we'll try to stop the bleeding."

Joe, who was just leaving for work, came back to help. We tried every remedy ever heard of to stop the flow of blood, but nothing had any effect. Cold compresses to the back of the neck, lying flat on the floor, and pinching his nostrils together, were all useless. We were later told that lying down was the worst thing he could have done, because it meant that he was swallowing most of the blood.

With Todd safely on the bus, we rushed Ken to the hospital. A day of painful tests followed, including one of the most excruciating, the bone marrow test. This procedure involved inserting a large needle into the chest bone and withdrawing some of the bone marrow, which is then examined under a microscope.

After the many tests were completed, our family doctor's diagnosis was confirmed. It was indeed, Purpura, a disease which was explained to us as being the opposite of Leukemia, with too many red blood cells and a decrease in the blood platelets.

Ken was admitted to the hospital immediately for treatment, and there followed a very hectic and worrying time for all of us. As with most of our family activities, everything had to be scheduled around Todd's needs, and now there was a lot of travel back and forth to the hospital. Someone had to be at home in the morning to see him on the bus, and again in the afternoon at three fifteen when he arrived home. I hated to think what might happen if the house was empty when he got off the bus.

He had recently graduated from antics in the bedroom to invading his father's workshop with catastrophic results. Paint, oil and tar were a few of his targets. He mixed them together as he had done in the past with his sisters' makeup, and spread masses of goo over tools and anything else in sight.

On one occasion he emptied a five gallon can of gasoline on the workshop floor, which we didn't realize until the fumes began seeping into the house. Luckily, it was summer, so we opened all the doors and windows and cleaned things up as best we could. There was no way of knowing what he might do next.

For three weeks while Ken was in the hospital, we juggled schedules, working on a shift basis. With barely enough time to prepare a decent meal, everyone became slightly frazzled, but with all members of the family cooperating, we weathered the storm.

At the end of the three weeks, Ken was allowed to return home, but there followed weekly visits to the hospital for checkups. He was treated with a drug called, "Prednesone", and the blood platelets gradually returned to normal. The treatments continued for six months until he was fully recovered.

This crisis had no more than reached a successful conclusion when I, myself, needed surgery which would mean a week's stay in the hospital. What was to be done about Todd? Certainly no one could be expected to stay home from work or school to be with him.

There seemed to be only one solution. As much as I didn't like the idea, the only answer was the drop-in centre at the psychiatric hospital. Children could be admitted there temporarily in an emergency situation.

So once more, arrangements were made. Todd would be admitted for one week, or for as long as I needed to remain in the hospital.

We drove there on a Sunday, the day I had to check in. We dropped Todd off on the way, and he and I both cried. I wondered if he thought I was leaving him for good this time, and there was no way to explain the situation to him in terms he would understand. So I told him I would be back for him as soon as I could, and I left him again.

Through the week that followed, he was on my mind constantly. The staff at the drop-in centre was in constant touch with me, which relieved my mind greatly. Through telephone calls and visits from staff members, I was assured that Todd was doing well, participating in educational and musical activities. Since he still loved music so much, I knew he would be enjoying that part of his stay.

My surgery went well, and I was released at the end of a seven day period. I don't know which of us was happier when we picked Todd up to take him home, but I did know that never again, no matter how bad things got, could I ever bring myself to place him in an institution permanently. Even though he received excellent care and was treated well, I would have no peace of mind.

I did wonder at times if it was fair to other family members to keep him at home. But I told myself that he was a family member, too, and he had the right to live as such. It was fortunate that his brothers and sisters loved him, even though he made things difficult for them at times.

It was shortly after we arrived back home from this experience when Grandpa moved in.

A mischievous Todd after our move to the country.

Life's always been "just ducky" as far as Todd's concerned!

With Pa—Grandpa Roberts.

With Mom August, 1984

With other Special Olympians. Todd is in the
back row, on the left.

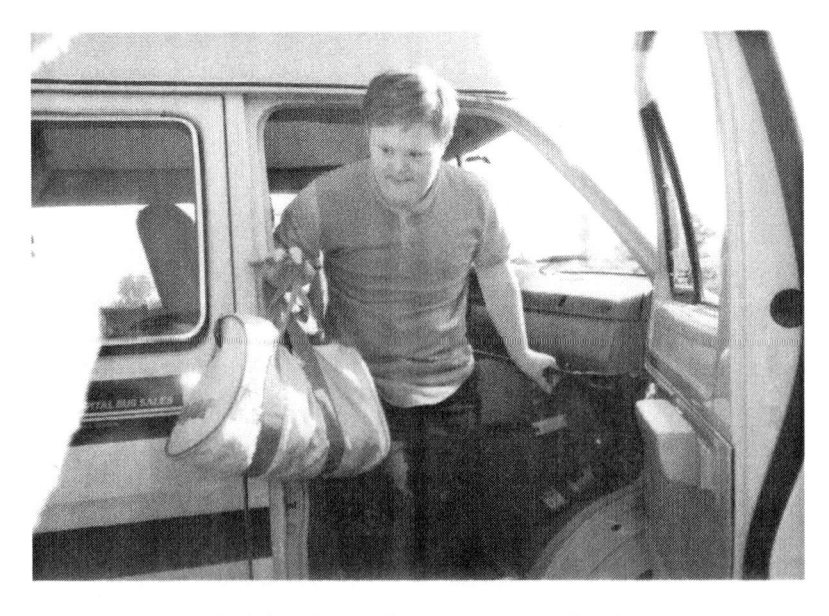

Arriving home from Morven School.

Tripping the light fantastic with his sister Becky at a family wedding.

Catching up with former Morven School alumni and friend Chris Parks.

Chapter 8

A Special Friendship

My father was eighty-one years old when the question was raised of his coming to live with us. An old war injury made it difficult for him to walk without the aid of a cane, and I was uncertain as to how well it would work out having him with us. I must admit, I wasn't too happy about the idea.

Didn't I already have enough to contend with? Did everyone think I was some sort of superwoman to take on another person to care for, a person who would probably require more of my time than I had to give?

Having lived with one of my brothers in the city since my mother's death several years before, I knew why Dad was anxious to make a change at that particular time of his life. He had lived on this same farm in his younger years, working the fields from dawn until dusk every day, and he knew every inch of the land by heart. To him, it was already home, and several of his children had been born here. He only wanted to spend his remaining years in the surroundings he knew and loved. How could I turn my back on him? So I agreed to his proposal, and he moved in with our family.

That was the beginning of an unforgettable period in my life, and in Todd's as well. He accepted Grandpa without question, and they got along well enough after some initial adjustments on both sides. They soon became accustomed to each other's peculiarities, and grew quite fond of one another. In the beginning, Grandpa was "Pompa" to Todd, but soon he shortened it to "Pa", because it was much easier to pronounce.

Pa would reach for his cane on a warm summer day and go for a stroll around the big yard. That was Todd's signal to race after him, running in wide circles around Pa's unsteady steps. I feared, at times, that he would be knocked off his feet, but he struggled staunchly onward. Once in a while he'd pause to rest, reaching out playfully with his cane as though he meant to catch Todd around the neck with it.

"Run into me, will you, you little devil?" he grumbled good-naturedly, "I'll fix you, me boy!"

Todd would burst into frenzied laughter, and was gone in a flash, out of reach of the wooden cane. Later, when they were both tired out from this activity, Pa would come into the house and drop down in his chair, and Todd would climb onto his lap. Todd could say only a few words and form no sentences, but the two of them were able to communicate in their own way. In spite of such a hectic time, it was wonderful to watch this relationship, and at such times I wondered why I'd worried so much about Pa coming to live with us.

That's not to say that things always ran smoothly, and sometimes I didn't know if I was coming or going. Often they both needed me at the same time, or I'd be helping Pa with something, and Todd would disappear, and I'd have to drop everything to go looking.

Todd had a sunny, happy disposition most of the time, except when he didn't get his own way, and then he could become very stubborn and angry. Digging in his heels and spewing forth a stream of unintelligible words, the object of his wrath was apt to be the target of various flying objects. We were all on the receiving end from time to time.

He loved to imitate, and was able to remember many television ads and situations. He could send everyone into gales of laughter as he re-enacted scenes he'd watched on the screen.

One of his favourite television shows was "Good Times", a comedy featuring a black family struggling to get by in the big city. Todd was partial to a character named, "J.J.", who was forever getting himself into impossible situations, and made things difficult in general for the rest of the family. Perhaps, in his own way, Todd felt a certain connection with "J.J.", and sympathized with his problems.

"J.J." was a tall, gangling youth, easy-going, and happy go lucky. After every successful caper, he had a habit of swaggering across the screen, arms raised in front, palms down. Then he'd wave his arms back and forth in an exaggerated manner, roll his eyes and exclaim, "Dy-no-mite!"

One afternoon, Pa and I were relaxing with a cup of tea, when Todd did his famous disappearing act. I didn't worry too much, as I knew he was somewhere in the house. Taking much pleasure in this rare moment of inactivity, I was content to take full advantage of it.

Suddenly, a strange apparition appeared in the kitchen doorway. I stared, dumbfounded. I knew it must be Todd, but every inch of his arms and face was as black as coal.

Advancing slowly into the kitchen in typical "J.J." fashion with arms raised in the air before him, Todd smiled broadly. The black face showed his small, white teeth to perfection as he proudly announced, "I J.J . . . Dy-o-my!"

Speechless, I finally rose and walked slowly toward him. As I came closer to where he was standing, the unmistakable odor of shoe polish filled my nostrils.

He could tell that Pa and I were properly impressed when we broke up into shouts of laughter. Pa thought it was very creative and imaginative, and had the best laugh of all.

"He's not so dumb," Pa said when he had caught his breath, "He's a smart boy!"

Todd stubbornly refused to allow the shoe polish to be wiped off. "No, no!" he insisted, "I J.J.!"

He was, however, eventually convinced that even his hero J.J. got cleaned up sometimes, and since his daily bath was an established ritual, the shoe polish was finally removed.

This incident proved to me that his thought processes were much more normal than most people gave him credit for. He had approached a problem in a unique fashion. To him, it was easy. He needed something to make himself black, and he found that something in the form of black shoe polish.

My father lived with us for two years, and seemed to enjoy himself most of the time in spite of all the commotion. When he was eighty-four, he suffered a stroke which left his legs and right side paralyzed, making it very difficult to care for him at home. He was confined to a wheelchair for the rest of his life and, much as I disliked the idea, he eventually had to be admitted to a nursing home in order to receive the care he needed.

He hated it there, and never felt that he belonged there. He never thought of himself as old or feeble. Every time we went to visit, he was sitting alone in his chair at the end of the long hall, gazing down the corridor, just waiting for someone to come. I think he deliberately chose that position so that he could see his visitors as soon as they rounded the corner. He always asked after Todd, his lonely blue eyes coming to life for a moment.

"Where's the boy?" he'd demand, "Why don't you ever bring him to see me?"

So once or twice we took Todd with us, but it was no place for a little whirlwind like him.

Sometimes we'd take Pa home with us for the weekend, and those were the times he looked most forward to.

On Sunday he'd ask, "Say, do you think you'll be having any company today?"

He was in his glory when any of our married children came to visit. "The more the merrier!" he always said. He teased Todd, who still took great delight in tantalizing Pa, as always, snatching his glasses or cane and hiding them somewhere in the house.

It was shortly after his eighty-sixth birthday that Pa died, and I was happy that he had been with us for a while. When I show his photograph to Todd, he still remembers. He gazes at it for a second or two, smiles and says, "Pa!"

It is good that these two, one at the end of his life and the other just beginning his, knew the pleasure of one another's company. It should always be so between grandfathers and grandsons.

Chapter 9

Everything Happens For A Reason

Along with the gladness I felt because my father had been with us for a time, there was also a sense of loss, and some self-recrimination. Had I done everything possible for him, or could I have given more of my time and caring? At the time, I believed I was doing everything I could, and all that was expected of me. He had lived a long and difficult life, and well-meaning friends said, "You have nothing to feel guilty about. Everything happens for the best, and life goes on."

It wasn't that death was a new acquaintance of mine. A mother, sister, a tiny granddaughter, and several other relatives and close friends were gone from my life, and I was tired of watching people die; but it was more than that.

Each time I lost someone close to me, each time I stood beside another grave, a little piece of my life went with them. That part of life shared with them was gone forever, leaving an empty place behind.

That emptiness must be filled with someone or some thing, and I tried to fill this one with a quest to search out life's why's and wherefores, its reasons and rationale. So it was that my interest was aroused in inspirational books by authors like Norman Vincent Peale, and I pursued these works diligently.

As my search for answers continued, I began to believe there is a reason behind everything that happens in our lives, and that we learn something necessary to our growth as individuals from each new experience.

It made a great deal of sense. Look how much I'd learned from Todd, even as I was trying to teach him. He'd taught me awareness, compassion, tolerance, understanding, acceptance and love, and I wondered if what I was learning from him wasn't more important than what I was trying to teach. Perhaps I had been too absorbed with self, and needed to consider and serve others more. Because of him, I would never again be able to ignore or scorn anyone less fortunate than myself.

Doctor Peale's ideas were interesting and novel to me. Some of them I found helpful and enjoyable, for I was open to any suggestions that would have a positive effect.

He wrote, "Every night before going to sleep, mentally gather all of your worries, problems, and negative thoughts. Toss the whole works over the side of the bed, and then forget them. You can't do anything about them until morning, anyway."

You know, it really worked! There were many opportunities to put this theory to the test, and some nights there was a lot to throw away. Let me tell you, the floor on my side of the bed really took a beating!

Doctor Peale also advocated making quiet times for oneself, to find a time and place to be absolutely alone and let the mind go blank, shutting out the world completely.

This last part was more difficult to do, but I discovered that the best time for me was either late at night after everyone else was in bed, or very early in the morning. Practicing this advice daily brought added peace and strength for dealing with stressful situations, and eventually, the bedroom floor on my side of the bed received less punishment.

All this doesn't mean that the problems and heartaches disappeared miraculously overnight, or that there was a phenomenal change in everyday life. However it did help improve my outlook, so it was worth it. There was less self pity, and fewer "whys". There were, however, still doubts and dissatisfactions.

Todd appeared to be happy enough, but I guess I wanted more for him than reality would allow. There were so many mountains still to climb, so many compromises to make. I'd watch other mothers with children much younger than Todd, and they were leaving us behind.

Todd's own nieces and nephews were outgrowing him in every way except physically. In the beginning, his interests had closely paralleled theirs concerning playthings and work they brought home from school to be proudly displayed on the door of the fridge. Theirs progressed from printing to writing; and from colouring traced pictures to inventing their own drawings.

Todd was still printing his first name in an unsteady hand, and going over the lines of his crayon coloured pictures supplied by the school. They went up on the fridge door, anyway, and he was as proud as if they had been painted by Vincent Van Gogh. In reality, I knew all this was to be expected, but I kept looking for some sort of breakthrough.

He'd toss his work on the table in front of me with a flourish and a happy grin when he came home from school.

"Mom, look! Work!"

"That's so good, Todd. Did you do that picture all by yourself?"

"Yeh."

"Well, I think that should go on the fridge. It's such a pretty colour."

"Kay."

That was all it took to make him happy. A snowman might hang on the fridge door until July, because he noticed if it was taken down. A colorful apple tree with one red apple on the ground underneath stayed put for an entire year, and I missed it myself when it finally had to be removed.

There were some small victories. He had learned approximately twenty words by sight using the flash card system; simple words like "girl", "boy", "play", "come", "go", etc. At least it was occasion for a little rejoicing.

He found happiness in small things, and I began to view things through his eyes. Something as routine as eating out in a restaurant was special to him. He was impressed with everything, including the light fixtures. A sparkling chandelier would catch his attention.

"Mom, look. Light . . . pretty!"

"Yes, Todd. It is pretty, isn't it?"

"Eight light, Mom."

Eight was his favourite number. When asked how old he was, the answer was always eight. At dinner time he wanted eight potatoes, and on bowling day he always got eight strikes. There were eight kids on his bus, and he had eight teachers at school. He was partial to sports jerseys, and they always had to be numbered with an "eight".

He was also intrigued with the fact that he had two glasses to drink from in the restaurant, one containing water, and the other filled with Coca Cola, which was his favourite drink. Then he'd begin counting again.

"Eight drink, Mom."

"No, Todd. You only have two drinks, water and Coke."

Then his attention would be drawn by something else, perhaps the colourful wallpaper. It had become possible to keep him calmed down long enough to take him to public places more often, but he wasn't the only one who was becoming more settled. I was more relaxed and accepting of the fact that I had a son who was very different, and that it would always be so. I didn't mind as much when people stared, and I was beginning to enjoy being with him. His happy, carefree personality gave me many moments of pleasure.

He loved playing cards, even though he couldn't understand the different suits or their value. The two of us often played a game of high card. We'd each turn up a card from our hand, and the highest numbered card won both. I'd tell him which of us had won, and his delight knew no bounds if his pile of cards was larger than mine when the game was over. Often he'd just sit very still for an hour at a time, letting the cards slide through his fingers, as though spellbound by the colourful display.

There weren't many things he was afraid of. He didn't like to stand underneath a tree, but he could go outdoors on a dark summer evening and find his way around the yard with no problem. Going after him when I felt uneasy about him being outside alone, I always walked into something. When I cried out, he'd squeal with delight. He was invisible in the darkness, so I'd call his name, trying to find out where he was by the direction of his voice.

"Todd, come and help me. I hurt my foot and I can't see where I am!"

Silence would follow, and there'd be a faint giggle.

"Hurry up, Todd, come and help me. I hurt my foot!"

Another moment of silence, and then he'd come dashing out from behind the barn, or from the back of the house saying, "Be kay, Mom, be kay."

On one such outing I found him quite a distance from the house. I heard the beep of his Star Trek communicator button, and I asked him what he was doing.

"Be me up!" he answered, in a tone of voice that questioned why I would wonder such a thing. He was quite disappointed that he hadn't suddenly been transported to the mythical "Starship Enterprise". I explained to him that you only got beamed aboard when you were in real danger. I'm sure he would have enjoyed conversing with his two favourite characters, Mr. Chekov and Mr. Spock.

Occasionally, I wondered what on earth I'd spent my time at before he came into my life, and how I'd occupy myself if he wasn't around. I hoped I'd never have to find out.

Chapter 10

A Young Man Blossoms

The year that Todd turned nine, we had two weddings in the family. Heather and Joe were married within a month of each other, Heather to Bill Wilson, and Joe to Debbie Bald. Terry became engaged to Bonnie Mayhew that same year. The children were gradually moving ahead to start homes and families of their own.

What a summer that was! With wedding showers, shopping, and wedding plans to finalize, it was a hectic time. And with Todd out of school for the summer, he didn't get the same amount of attention and supervision that he usually did. I wouldn't go so far as to say he ran wild, but he came pretty close to it.

I worried beforehand how his behaviour would hold up during the church ceremonies, but it was better than I imagined it would be. He attempted to sing along with the soloist at one wedding, but the guests generously overlooked it.

At the second wedding, he insisted on tapping and banging his new shoes on the floor and the back of the seat ahead of him as he very quickly became bored with the proceedings. That was a little more difficult to ignore, but we made it through that trial, as well.

The dances following the weddings were more to his liking. He had a good sense of rhythm, and was happy just dancing by himself.

After Heather and Joe moved into their own homes, there were minor adjustments all around. We were busy for a time playing musical rooms, and everyone ended up with different sleeping quarters.

It's a strange but true thing. When children leave home they always seem to take things you wish they'd leave behind, and leave things you wish they'd take. Don't ever be foolhardy and throw anything away, for as sure as you do, they'll come and ask for it the following day.

Our family collection began at that time, and has steadily mounted through the years. There is one small room upstairs where all those miscellaneous objects have accumulated. Broken stereos, books, school papers, pet rocks, photographs, autograph books, old boots and shoes, to name a few. Perhaps some day I'll load it all up and deliver it to the rightful owners!

A couple of years after she was married, Heather became pregnant. When her doctor discovered she had a Down's brother, he recommended that she consult a genetics specialist at Kingston General Hospital.

Recent research into the condition had disclosed that there are actually two forms of the Syndrome. There is "Trisonary Twenty-One," for which there appears to be no apparent reason other than the mother's age. The second type is known as "Translocation", when the mother has a chromosome with an extra piece attached. In this instance the mother may have a Down's child and the condition may be passed on through another child to their children.

The specialist requested permission to perform a simple blood test on Todd which would determine if his type was translocation, which could be passed on to Heather's child.

At the time of Todd's birth it was not known that there was a second type of the Syndrome. Angela and Maureen each had two normal children, and I had no idea that there was the slightest possibility of Down's being passed on to any of my children's children. I knew that having the test done would ease Heather's mind as well as mine, and gave permission.

A week later, Heather, Todd and I drove into the city to meet with the specialist. It turned out to be quite a day. The test itself was a very simple procedure and was soon over. It proved conclusively that Todd's type was indeed "Trisonary Twenty-One", and could not be passed on to my children's children. Needless to say, we were relieved and very happy.

The physician asked if we would be willing to meet with some other doctors who were studying Down's Syndrome, as they were interested in asking some questions regarding our experiences involving Todd. Since we were already in the hospital, we agreed, and were ushered into a room, a sort of amphitheater, with rows of seats rising behind and above each other with an open area in front.

Much to our surprise, the seats were filled with young doctors. We were a little shocked, as we hadn't expected such a crowd. I, for one, had never before seen so many white coats in one place at the same time.

Of course, all eyes were on us, and Todd thoroughly enjoyed the fact that he was the centre of attention. A few questions were directed to him, but for once, he was quiet, covering his face with his hands and peeking through his fingers. In spite of feeling somewhat out of place, and a little too much in the spotlight, we answered their questions as best we could.

Among other things, they were interested in knowing if I had experienced any special problems during my pregnancy or delivery. They were also curious as to how Todd related to other family members, and how we, as a family, dealt with the problems of his handicap.

Then a query was tossed in my direction that I was hard put to answer.

"Mrs. Wilkinson", the specialist asked, "If the amniocentesis test had been available during your pregnancy and had shown that your baby was abnormal, would you have terminated the pregnancy, or carried your baby to term?"

Everyone waited expectantly for my answer. Before Todd was born, it might not have been such a difficult question, but there he stood—my loving, affectionate, special son, smiling at me happily, as though awaiting my answer along with the doctors. I recalled all the experiences we'd shared, the happy and not so happy times. Times when, through my ignorance and lack of faith I'd asked, "Why?", and I was thankful I had not been forced to make such a decision all those years before.

"I'm really not sure," I finally replied, "I guess I'd have to be faced with that situation before I could give you an honest answer."

Things had changed a lot since that day so long ago when I'd thought it was the end of the world for me, and perhaps I had changed most of all. And one thing is certain. If I were asked that same question again today, I now know what my answer would be. I would have my baby.

During this time, things were going quite well for Todd at school. He was printing his first name and part of his surname, and was learning to count to ten. He was also working at telling time, and the identification of coins, but progress in this area was very slow. Both at school and at home we were working with him on tying his shoelaces, but he was also finding this very difficult.

For a couple of weeks he'd been coming home every day in a very happy and excited mood, reeling off a stream of words that, to us, were unintelligible. After it was repeated several times and we were still unable to understand, he became very frustrated and turned away impatiently muttering, "Oh, ne'er mine!" (never mind)

To someone with normal children, this may not seem like a big deal, but parents of children like Todd will understand how upsetting and complicated this situation can be. It is frustrating for the child, yes, but equally so for the parents. Just try to imagine what it would be like if your child was not able to tell you what happened at school on a certain day; what he did, what he wanted to do, or things the teacher had said.

You will understand, then, that my heart went out to Todd, and I could understand his frustration and disappointment. Here he was, trying his best to tell us something that was obviously important to him, and none of us had the faintest idea what it was all about.

This went on for several days in a row, and finally I talked with the teachers at school, repeating the words the way they sounded to us. Everyone there was as much in the dark as we were, and the mystery was no closer to being solved.

Then one day, a letter was sent home concerning the Special Olympics that would soon be taking place. This is the annual sporting competition for mentally handicapped people, and since Todd had reached the age of twelve, he was now qualified to compete. I was excited and happy for him.

"Oh", I exclaimed, "You're going to the Special Olympics!"

"Yeh!" he grinned, his face lighting up as his smile spread from ear to ear.

And then, as if a great load had been lifted from his shoulders, he began waving his arms in the air and repeated the now familiar words that he'd been trying for so long to make us understand. "Special Olympics." The great mystery was solved.

The Special Olympics was a wonderful experience for all the participating students. Schools in each area had a mini Olympic event in which they competed against one another, and the winners in each of those events went on to compete in the Canada-wide Olympics.

The students practiced for months, looking forward with great anticipation to June, when the event took place. The activity and enthusiasm gradually built to a frenzied climax, which culminated on the awesome day.

The opening ceremonies were a thrilling, stirring experience, not only for the participants, but for parents, teachers, and casual spectators as well. Students from each school, attired in sports outfits in individual school colours, paraded around the field, preceded by a band of Scottish Highlanders in their colourful kilts, and marching smartly along to the rousing strains of the bagpipes. Two athletes from each school proudly bore their school banner aloft, to the accompaniment of excited cheering and applauding. Morven School's colours were yellow and green, and as the different events were taking place around the field, those colours stood out like a beacon to those of us who were cheering for them. For many of the parents it meant travelling quite some distance to another town or city for this very special occasion. It was well worth the trip, though, and there was always someone from our family to cheer Todd on.

He didn't break any record, that's for sure, but there was great happiness for him to be involved, and for us to be there to watch. He'd always been a good runner, but when a race actually began, he was so occupied looking behind to see how his performance was affecting us, he usually fell far behind in the competition.

"Go, Todd, go!" we'd scream. He'd grin happily and move a little faster. Once, in a spurt of speed, one of his shoes flew into the air. Grinding to a halt to recover it, he lost precious time and finished last in that particular race. He didn't mind. He was having the time of his life.

I often thought of the Special Olympics slogan, "Let me win, but if I cannot win, let me be brave in the attempt". These participants were all brave, all proud, and all worthy.

The first year Todd participated, his only claim to fame was a participation ribbon and a Special Olympics t-shirt. However, he was as proud and happy as someone who had won a gold medal. We, his family, were every bit as proud as the family of any athlete who participates in any Olympic competition anywhere, and his being there was one more step up the mountain. It was a step that I had never, in my wildest dreams, imagined or thought possible.

I was reminded again of the words of the doctor in the beginning, telling me that there would be joys and there would be sorrow. I'll say one thing about the joys. They weren't just little joys. They were moments of unbelievable happiness, wiping away many tears of sorrow.

The Special Olympics usually lasted for two days, and when we arrived home, the experience was re-lived as we informed family members who had not been able to attend. The high jump would have to be demonstrated, as was the broad jump, the football kick, and the ball toss.

"Come on, Todd; show us how fast you ran! How high you jumped!"

Todd happily obliged. This was his chance to impress, and he took full advantage.

Every year after that first one, the rest of us looked forward to the Special Olympics as much as he did. He won a few ribbons now and then, and that was good enough as far as he was concerned. It was good enough for us, too. After all, he was the only member of the family who had ever made it to the Olympics!

It's true, he wore no wreath of laurel leaves like some famous athletes in history, but in my heart he was crowned with glory, and I was warmed by the glow.

When Todd turned twelve, he was also eligible to attend summer camp at Roblin Lake in Picton, Ontario. This was sponsored by the Salvation Army, and lasted for two weeks. Young people, our daughter Becky among them, were employed as counselors, and it was a fun time for all. There were crafts and canoeing and of course, swimming.

It was the type of life that Todd favored, especially the swimming. He returned home sunburned and wind blown, but happy. I guess he didn't stay still long enough to have sun block applied.

We missed him while he was away, but knew that this was a part of life that he needed to experience. After all, don't all kids go to camp?

Chapter 11

A Troubled Teen

There was no grade system at Morven School as in other elementary schools. Instead, students were assigned to different levels according to age, beginning with primary class, junior intermediate and senior rooms.

At age fifteen, Todd was in the intermediate room, and was progressing as well as could be expected. I tried to keep in contact with the teachers and principal as closely as possible, which was necessary for all concerned.

Through parent-teacher interviews and written reports, parents were kept informed as to their child's progress. I blessed the school and teachers many times over, and wondered what I would have done if they hadn't been there. If I had a particular problem with Todd at home, it was helpful to make the teachers aware of it, and they were often able to help.

At one point, for instance, he developed the habit of switching on the stove burners, and had to be watched closely in order to avoid a potentially dangerous situation. When it was drawn to the attention of his home room teacher, all the students were given a lesson as to what could happen if they tried to operate an electric stove when they didn't know how to use it properly. It seemed to work for Todd, and once more, a problem was behind us.

The following year, there were many changes at the school. Some students left, new ones arrived, along with a new principal and teacher. Combined with Todd's teenage years, all these events may have played a part in altering the situation. For whatever reason, Todd began having problems at school.

Looking back, it's difficult to tell exactly what the reasons were, or when they really began. Perhaps it was a combination of things. Call it a personality conflict perhaps, but he and his new teacher were like oil and water together, and the problems apparently were there for some time before I was aware of them.

I realized one day that Todd wasn't being his usual happy, smiling self when he returned home at the end of the school day. Throwing his lunch pail aside, and without pausing for his after-school snack, he'd stomp upstairs, banging his feet on each step as he went. At first, when I questioned him, he'd pull away, scowling, and mutter, "Ne'er mine! Lea' me 'lone!"

The first few times it happened, I supposed it was a case of a bad day that most of us experience from time to time. When it had been going on for two or three weeks, though, I began to worry.

"What's the matter, Todd? Did something happen at school?"

"No!"

Then I'd hear crashing and banging upstairs, as he threw anything and everything that wasn't nailed down, often breaking small ornaments, and once it was a lamp. Something had to be done. I had to find out what was causing this upset.

I called his teacher and heard some disturbing things that didn't sound like Todd at all. He'd been punished several times and disciplined on numerous occasions. I had no quarrel with discipline when called for, but didn't agree with the kind I was hearing about.

Sometimes, the teacher told me, if his work wasn't finished on time, Todd wasn't allowed his mid-morning snack. On one occasion, because exercise time in the gym took place at the end of the school day, he was sent out to his bus without his pants on because he was too slow changing from his gym uniform. The idea, apparently, was that this punishment would cause him so much embarrassment that he would finish dressing on time thereafter.

I heard of other incidents, as well. The teacher gave him the nickname, "Toad", and called him a baby. She said he tore pages out of his work book, and this wasn't at all like him, because he was always so proud of his work, especially if he was given a little praise.

Once more he was pleading to stay home from school. "Me 'tay home, Mom, pease? Be good, work, do dishes. Pease?"

"You know you have to go to school, Todd. What ever's wrong, we'll fix it, and make it right, okay?"

"Kay."

That night, when I tucked him in bed, my protective instincts took over when I saw such a sad, worried look on his face, and I girded myself for battle. I toyed with the idea of keeping him at home permanently, but this course of action would undo everything he'd accomplished so far. The situation had to be remedied, for I could not accept the unhappiness he was experiencing, and my own state of anxiety.

To say I vehemently disagreed with the teacher's methods of discipline is putting it mildly. I knew there were occasions when Todd could be stubborn and uncooperative, but I also knew him well enough to know that the methods being used would never work with him. I later found out that this teacher had previously taught only "normal" children, so that explained part of the problem. However, if this was the case, I did not understand why she was teaching at Morven School at all.

Todd and his teacher were having their problems, and I was having mine. However to me, Todd's problems were the most important. He couldn't tell me what was happening with him, so all I had to go by was his continuing upsetting behaviour at home, and reports of rebellious incidents at school. Then he resorted to hiding various items of his clothing around the school. I decided to go to Morven to talk with both his teacher, and the principal, but first I resorted to an action I had never before considered taking. I made a call to the Board of Education to report what was happening.

The Board member who was responsible for the students at Morven set up an appointment to meet with Frank and myself, along with Todd's teacher. In the meantime, I had suggested that the gym period could perhaps be held earlier in the day to avoid the delay in dressing and being slow to catch the bus. I was told that Todd's teacher knew how to handle the problem better than I.

When we met for the appointment, the teacher repeated the problems and her methods of discipline. I informed them that I had wondered about keeping Todd at home, hoping this would help them realize how upset and angry I was. The Board member advised against that action, saying we'd try something less drastic first.

The result was that Todd was placed in another room with a different teacher, and the situation slowly began to improve. I was grateful, the furniture was grateful, and I'm sure the teacher was just as happy.

She and I never discussed the matter again. Although we did remain on fairly friendly terms, the friendship was a guarded one.

I was very happy we had all weathered the storm, and also that Todd was looking forward to boarding the school bus again each morning. Let's face it, at the age he had reached, I could no longer forcibly pull his clothes on and carry him out to the bus myself. He was almost big enough to carry me!

A few months later, a very significant incident occurred. I woke up one morning, looked at the clock, and realized immediately that we had overslept.

Todd's bus would have left ten minutes earlier. I flew into his room to find his bed empty. Frank followed me downstairs, both of us calling his name as we went. The kitchen was empty, too, and Frank ran outdoors to look. We thought Todd had probably gone outside to play as he often did.

There was no sign of him anywhere. I was beginning to panic now, wondering if he had wandered away, or even fallen into the creek. Back in the kitchen, Frank and I looked at each other in dismay. Why hadn't he wakened us? Where could he be?

"You don't suppose," I said, "That he somehow managed to get on the bus by himself, do you?" Even as I was voicing the words, I felt it was a pretty remote idea.

"No," Frank answered quickly, "He could never get ready all by himself, or make his own lunch. And he wouldn't know when to go out to catch the bus!"

"Well, we'll have to do something! I'll have to call the school and let them know what's going on."

My hands were shaking as I dialed the number. I explained the situation, and, hoping against hope, asked if he hadn't, by any chance, made it to school.

"Just a minute, we'll have a look," the principal answered. I waited impatiently while a teacher checked the bus, which had just arrived. Frank, meanwhile, was still searching in case we had overlooked something.

"Yes, he's here," the principal's voice informed me a few minutes later, and a wave of relief swept over me. I couldn't believe that he had actually done it all by himself.

"Thank goodness!" I exclaimed. "What's he wearing?"

"Black leather shoes, track pants and a t-shirt. He's got his lunch pail, and there's a jam sandwich and a piece of cake in it. Don't worry, we'll make sure he gets some lunch."

As I hung up the receiver, I looked at Frank in amazement. I would never have believed he was capable of such an accomplishment. Later, we found the remains of his breakfast on a small table in the front porch—a glass containing a little juice, and a few cake crumbs on a plate. Not a very nutritious start to the day, but I was feeling elated and very proud.

That was how the pattern seemed to go—a "down" time, followed by some incident so encouraging that I felt like celebrating. That little critter with feathers was certainly getting his exercise!

It seemed like only yesterday Todd had been the youngest student at Morven, devilish and unpredictable, unwilling to even talk about getting ready for school. Not that he wasn't still unpredictable, but that day, in my opinion, he had exonerated himself somewhat, and wiped the slate clean. He was growing up, and I was a little nostalgic, wondering where the time had gone.

As in all families, there were changes continually taking place. By now, Debby had married Harry Cutler and moved into her own home. Although she was only ten miles away, I missed her, and of course, so did Todd. She had always been one of his staunchest allies, almost like a second mother.

In the past, whenever he had found himself in difficulty, Debby was the person he ran to if I was unsympathetic. She showered him with affection, and he returned that affection fully, often preferring her company over mine.

"Come on, Todd," I'd tell him, "I'll get your bath ready."

"No, Bebby do it," was the reply.

"But Debby's busy."

"Bebby do!" he'd insist, a little more emphatically, so Debby usually did.

When he was very young, his pronunciation of her name was "Bebby", and as he grew older, it became more of a habit, I think, than the fact that he was unable to pronounce the name correctly.

With Debby gone, I only had three helpers left at home. Ken and Dave, both out of school, had jobs, and Becky was in high school. Todd had left many of his former habits behind, and was moving at a slightly slower pace, but as one trait was abandoned, another sprung into being.

The towel over the head was replaced by a cloth in the hand, which he twirled and swung, sometimes wrapping it between his fingers until it eventually twisted into nothing more than a kind of rope or string. My dish towels were often a target for this activity, and if I reclaimed the one in current use after he was in bed, it was the first thing he asked for in the morning. Then he'd search frantically, and if it couldn't be found, he'd grab another one when I wasn't looking.

The one name he had no problem pronouncing was "Becky", and being closer in age to her than any of his other brothers and sisters, they had a few more things in common, too. One of those interests was their love of music. When the stereo was turned up full blast, and Becky said, "Come on, Todd, let's dance!" the house trembled.

They're both still as hooked on it as they ever were, and it turned into Becky's lifetime career. She eventually enrolled in the Radio Broadcasting course at Loyalist College in Belleville, and became a radio announcer. Her work-related travels would later take her from New

Brunswick and Prince Edward Island in the east, to Ontario, Alberta, and back to Ontario again.

Todd and his classmates were once treated to a tour of radio station C.F.F.X. in Kingston, where Becky was employed at the time, and were able to see, first hand, where the music they listened to originated from. Music was one of the subjects they studied at school, and some of the students were surprisingly knowledgeable about music and performers.

When Todd was seventeen, David married Dorothy Dickson, and this provided another golden opportunity for Todd to demonstrate his dancing skills. During the reception, he disappeared from our table to the other end of the dance floor, and for the next few hours, all I could see of him was his yellow shirt through the crowd of dancers. There he was, doing the bird dance, which I had no idea he had ever seen before.

His lack of communication skills was no barrier to acquiring dance partners. One of Dorothy's relatives, whom he had never met before, was a favourite, and he gave her no rest.

He'd approach her table, point his finger at her, and say, "You, dance!" She knew what he meant, and she never refused.

At one point in the evening, Frank touched my arm and pointed toward the bar. I glanced up to see Todd and his partner waiting their turn to be served. My anxiety level reached a new peak.

"Good Lord!" I muttered, "I'd better get over there before things get out of hand!" Frank caught my arm.

"Leave him alone, he'll be alright." I remembered all the occasions prior to this when I'd heard those same words. I sat down again, against my better judgment. As I watched anxiously, Todd pointed to a bottle of ginger ale sitting on the bar, and I breathed a sigh of relief. Later, I attempted to persuade him to join the family at our table, but he pulled away.

"No, Mom, dance!" Then he was on the move again with that frenzied bird dance, doing as well at it as everyone else. Perspiration was streaming down his face, but the smile he wore was beautiful to behold, so who was I to burst his bubble?

When we arrived home at one-thirty in the morning, he was almost too exhausted to climb the stairs. His shoes were actually hot to the touch, but he'd had the time of his life.

"Come on, Todd, let's get you to bed." For the first time that evening, he was agreeable to one of my suggestions.

"Kay, Mom," he consented, and his weary feet carried him off to dreamland.

Chapter 12

Considering Options

Todd's attendance at Morven School prompted me to become a member of the local Association for the Mentally Handicapped. I was urged on in this role by other parents who were themselves playing active parts in the group. I welcomed it as an opportunity to do something constructive for others like Todd. I felt that it would also benefit him in many ways, and it was a gratifying feeling to be working with members of the Association who were very dedicated, caring individuals.

All members functioned on a volunteer basis, and as in all such groups, it was often a thankless task, and difficult to persuade people to become involved. There always seems to be more to do than there are hands to do it, but still, the work moves forward. Little by little, the barriers of misunderstanding and prejudice are being broken down as more and more of the handicapped are taking their rightful place in the community.

Living in group homes under the supervision of trained personnel, attending rehabilitation workshops each day, they have access to recreational facilities and a more normal way of life.

Our own Association, in conjunction with the Ministry of Community and Social Services, was able to greatly improve conditions in our area.

A group home was established, housing eight adult clients, and afterward, a new, modern rehabilitation workshop was built to replace the former, out-of-date structure. With forty clients in attendance, many areas of work experience were covered, from sewing to furniture re-finishing.

It has always bothered me to hear the mentally handicapped referred to as "retarded". The term is not used in relation to physically handicapped individuals who are usually referred to as "handicapped" or "impaired", and perhaps this accounts for the fact that there seems to be more prejudice toward mental as opposed to physical illness. With this in mind, the local Association worked on the problem and a vote was called for regarding a name change for our people.

Petitions were circulated throughout the community, as in other areas, and reaction was very favorable. The petitions were then forwarded to the proper authorities, and agreed to in principle. It was requested that Associations should present suitable names to choose from. This process was lengthy, but at the time of this writing, "Association for Community Living" is favored.

In the beginning, mention was made of the fact that costs would be too exorbitant to make the name change. Costs would involve paper work, changing of official letterheads, etc. This type of thinking filled me with great anger, for it appeared as though the mentally handicapped were being pushed aside and ignored for mainly financial reasons. It is high time that their rights and feelings are taken into consideration.

So, what of the future for people like Todd? What will be best for him? I only hope I have the courage to make the right decision on his behalf. Institutionalization doesn't even have a place in my thinking, but when his father and I are no longer able to cope, where will Todd's place be then? At the present time we are functioning quite well, I'm happy to say.

I wish we could live forever, but as the saying goes, "If wishes were horses, beggars would ride." We do not expect any of his brothers or sisters to care for him on a permanent basis. It would not be fair to them, for they each have their own families, their own responsibilities, and their own lives to live. It isn't that they haven't offered, but I believe time will show us the way.

At present, it would seem that a group home setting, with attendance at the workshop, would be suitable and acceptable. The family could still be close by, visit him, and have him home on weekends and holidays when possible. The important thing is that someone will be there to guide and love him.

I try not to worry about the future. It is easier to take one day at a time, to make the most of all that comes and the least of all that goes. There are so many mountains to climb, so many compromises to make.

As the doctor promised so long ago, I have come to accept. In the beginning, it was because I had to, but now it's because I want to. I have learned to accept and love, completely and without reservation, this unique personality known as Todd.

I still question some things, but now I have different questions. What is he thinking about when he sits outside on the porch steps on a warm summer day, gazing about at the sky and fields and trees? Since the expression on his face is so pleasing, I assume he is admiring his surroundings.

Does he dream at night, and what does he dream about? Does he, perhaps, dream that he has been beamed aboard the Starship Enterprise, and is soaring through space with his heroes? I like to think so.

I stopped asking "why" a long time ago. The "why" doesn't matter any longer, because I know there will never be an answer. What does matter is that we continue to move slowly forward, one step at a time. Each step takes us a little higher up the mountain, and as we climb, we'll make whatever compromises are necessary.

Chapter 13

A Time To Be Merry

On Christmas Eve, 1987, I sat alone, with only my thoughts for company. I thought of the year that was drawing to a close, and wondered what the New Year would bring.

It was almost midnight, and everyone else was in bed. Everything was quiet and peaceful, as the world waited in hushed expectancy for the excitement and hectic activity of the next day. Through the window, the Christmas lights on the small tree in front of the house shed their glow of red, green and blue across the snowy ground. I glanced out and searched the heavens for a star, but snow had begun to fall, and like the future, the night sky was hidden from view.

The large flakes fell gently, dropping straight down to spread a smooth, white blanket over the waiting world. It was surely such an evening, so white and still, that inspired the writing of "Silent Night".

The turkey was in a slow oven, its delicious aroma wafting its way into every corner of the house. I always start it cooking on Christmas Eve, and allow it to roast slowly through the night, because we prefer to eat at noon on Christmas Day. Maureen once said she loved coming home late on this special night of the year, for she knew the "smell" of Christmas would be the first thing to greet her when she opened the door.

The gifts were heaped under the tree, their colourful wrappings adding to the festivity of the season. The large, square one, right at the front of the pile, had Todd's name printed on it in large letters, so that he would see it as soon as he bounded into the living room in the morning. It was a Fisher Price "See-and-Spell" computer toy, recommended for children in the three to seven age group. Hopefully it would help him learn new words to extend his vocabulary. It's always difficult to know what type of gift will please Todd, and still be helpful to him at the same time. Even though his physical age was nineteen that Christmas, he was mentally in the seven year range—too old for many toys, and unable to appreciate adult things. (One exception to this rule was a mini-trampoline he received one year, and from which he derived many hours of pleasure.)

There were other gifts under the tree for him, of course. A hair dryer, toque and scarf, football shirt, pajamas, and a bulletin board for his room to hold all those precious awards he won at school. Everyone in the family bought gifts for him, so he always fared well.

Earlier that evening we'd attended church services. Todd enjoyed the carols and attempted to sing along, watching with interest as the Sunday school children re-enacted the journey to Bethlehem and the birth of Jesus. He would have enjoyed taking part, but would have looked out of place alongside the little ones.

On Christmas Day, most of the family would gather around the big dining room table for Christmas dinner. There would be about twenty-five of us, depending on how many could make the drive through the snow. We'd fill the table and overflow into the living room to find seats where ever we could. Any piece of furniture with a flat surface to accommodate a plate would serve as a table. One or two of the smaller children would be sure to spill their milk or juice, and probably some of their dinner, but it wouldn't matter. It was Christmas.

Everyone would eat too much, of course, and afterward, when the dishes were cleared away, we'd relax and visit. Remembering other Christmases, old times and old friends, Frank and I would say, as we often do, "Christmas isn't like it used to be when we were kids."

"We know," someone always replies good-naturedly, "You got one gift, and were glad to get it!"

"You're sure making up for it now," someone else will say, "Look at all the presents you got!"

Finally, a son or daughter will remark that, "It's been a great Christmas, Mom. Dinner was delicious. Maybe I'll have another piece of that pie before I go."

Then, one by one, each of our married children heads out the door into the cold winter evening with their families for the drive home. And each Christmas becomes a memory to be stored away for future reminiscing.

After everyone leaves, there's finally time to look at Todd's gifts with him again, delighting over one of his favourites. Perhaps he's offered help with a game or puzzle. He is content with such trivial things, never asking for much, and happy in his own world, somewhere between childhood, and the world of adults. It is a special world; one that only a few chosen people may enter, and I am privileged to share it with him.

Chapter 14

Time Flies

Todd attended Morven School until the age of twenty-one, then spent a year and a half at the Adult Rehabilitation Workshop, ARC Industries, in Napanee. At the end of that time, we decided it was better for him not to attend any longer. ARC contracts with various local businesses had been terminated because of closures, and there was no longer any productive work for him.

In 1995, a health problem surfaced. Todd suddenly became very withdrawn and listless. He was unable to sleep at night, and often sat on the upstairs hall floor most of the night, unmoving. His appetite failed, and as he began to lose weight, I was forced to spoon feed him. Even then, he ate very little. He completely lost interest in everything, even his music and television programs.

Our family physician was baffled as to what the problem might be, and we set up an appointment with a psychiatrist in Kingston.

After several visits, his diagnosis was depression, and he prescribed the drug "Zoloft". Within three weeks, Todd was well on his way to recovery. To date, there has been no relapse. There seemed to be no obvious reason for the depression but to me, it was yet another indication that people like Todd have the same moods and emotions as normal individuals. It was a happy time when this family problem was solved. The psychiatrist later told me that a short time after treating Todd, he had another Down's patient with the same symptoms, so there is a possibility that other Down's people may be susceptible to the condition.

In 1996, Becky was living and working as a radio announcer in Charlottetown, Prince Edward Island, and we were anxious to visit her. Early in September of that year, Todd, Frank and I boarded a plane in Ottawa for the flight there. I think Todd enjoyed the jet ride more than the rest of the tip, especially the flight after dark, with the many lights to be seen below us. In his mind, it was probably a Star Trek experience.

In April of 1998, Todd celebrated his thirtieth birthday, and had two caregivers, Karen and Heather. They took him out occasionally for recreational purposes, which he enjoyed very much.

With t.v. interests that included re-runs of "Little House on the Prairie", "Happy Days" and of course, "Star Trek", it seemed only natural for Todd to attend a trekkie convention in Toronto. Reservations were made in advance at the same hotel where the event was being held, and Heather accompanied Todd and I to the convention one sunny morning. It was a happy time. We rubbed shoulders with fierce looking Klingons and other Star Trek characters. Even William Shatner, a.k.a. "Captain Kirk" was there. We had our photo taken with the Klingons, and Todd bought himself a Star Trek jacket and watch with a replica of the Starship Enterprise on the dial.

Over the years, Todd has invested in an adult size trampoline, a swimming pool, and a basketball net. The latter hangs forlornly on the side of the barn because he is quite disinterested with it.

He loves books, even though he cannot read, but he pretends. He buys pencils by the dozen and scribbles his own kind of writing in his notebooks, but all he can really write is his name. When the page is full, he lays it in front of me so that I can tell him it is good work. With his love of books and writing, I often wonder who he might have become under different circumstances.

When we go shopping, Todd is very easy to please. Anything that is bright and colourful catches his eye, and he owns approximately twenty feather dusters in various shades. They stand handles down, in a wicker basket, so that they resemble a huge bouquet of bright flowers.

Although he is now in his late thirties, Todd is still a child in many ways, and it is difficult to treat him as an adult. I still tuck him into bed at night, kiss him on the forehead, and tell him I love him. Then he flashes his happy little smile and closes his eyes.

He and I are marching to a different drummer, and we're moving more slowly than the rest of the people in the parade because we pause so often to watch a pretty bird, or admire the beauty of a rainbow in the summer sky.

Sometimes I watch other mothers with their normal children. We aren't able to keep in step with them, and there's an ache in my heart for things that can never be. I'll never see Todd graduate from high school or college, go out on his first date, fall in love and get married. He'll never tell me his plans for the future, and he'll never have a family of his own.

As if sensing my sadness at such times, Todd smiles happily and takes my hand. He points to the sunshine flooding the room through the big window and says, "Mom, look! Pretty day!"

Suddenly, looking at his happy face, it doesn't matter if we are out of step with the rest of the world, and my heart feels the flutter of the "thing with feathers" again. The drummer is tapping out a joyful, lilting melody, and we're doing our best to keep time to the beat. Another quotation is echoing in my mind, drowning out the word "mongoloid", and it is this: "Weeping may endure for a night, but joy cometh in the morning."

It would be nice if we could finish the journey together, but time will not allow for such a fantasy, and reality tells me that my steps will come to a halt before his.

It will be difficult to leave him to finish the journey without me, but with a caring family to guide him, and God looking out for his own, I'll be leaving my son in good hands.

Our days are more serene now. Todd moves more slowly, but then, so do I. The other people in the parade are far out in front, but that's all right with us. The "thing with feathers" flutters in and out occasionally, and it is like an old friend now.

At this writing, Easter is almost here. As a new season of hope and joy is ushered in, may all Down's children and their parents rejoice in the knowledge that theirs is a unique and inspirational relationship, with God as a silent partner.

The End